This is Your Death

DOMINIC DEVINE

This is Your Death

St. Martin's Press
New York

Copyright © 1982 by Dominic Devine
For information, write: St. Martin's Press
175 Fifth Avenue, New York, N.Y. 10010
Manufactured in the United States of America

Library of Congress Cataloging in Publication Data

Devine, Dominic, 1920–
   This is your death. M

   I. Title.
PR6054.E9T47   1982   823′.914   82-5564
ISBN 0-312-80052-5   AACR2

First published in Great Britain by William Collins Sons & Co. Ltd.

PART I

CHAPTER 1

Julia's postcard took me by surprise. 'Looking forward to your visit,' it said. 'Ring and let us know when to expect you.'

Then I remembered Geoffrey's invitation. The previous November he had come down to my University to give a lecture on the contemporary novel. Mellowed by a good dinner in the Senior Common Room he had expansively invited me to spend part of my next summer vacation at Garston. It was the kind of invitation not meant to be taken seriously. Or so I had thought.

I phoned Julia that night. As I had guessed, there was an ulterior motive, which she scarcely bothered to conceal.

'Do you see much of Chris these days?' she asked, almost at once.

'From time to time,' I replied guardedly. I didn't want to discuss my son with Julia.

'Then you probably know that he and Anne'—Anne was her elder daughter—'want to get married?'

'Yes, I had a note from Chris last week.'

'It'll have to be stopped, of course,' she went on. 'It would never do . . .' Already Julia was getting my hackles up.

'So,' she added, 'as you're to be here anyway, we can get together on it.'

'What does Geoffrey think of the engagement?'

'Geoffrey? He's a broken reed. I'm afraid you'll find him changed, Maurice. He's become very odd.'

That was what decided me to accept the invitation to

Garston. I had heard vague rumours during the past months that all was not well with Geoffrey. Now was my chance to see for myself.

Geoffrey had built Garston in 1955, seven years ago. Before then he and Julia had lived first in Manchester and then in a flat in Bayswater. But Geoffrey had always wanted to live in the country and it didn't surprise me when I heard he had bought a piece of ground some thirty miles out of London. He sold his flat in London and used his Club any time he had to stay in town overnight.

The house stood in several acres of landscaped ground a mile or so west of the old village of Gleeve. You turned in through pillared gates and climbed a broad, shrub-lined avenue. A sharp left turn at the top and suddenly the rhododendrons were behind you and there was Garston, a long, low vision of glass and wood. It was a dramatic approach, impressive even on that wet, misty July afternoon when I first drove up. The place was eloquent of money — the immaculate lawns, the tennis court, the car-port sheltering a sleek black Daimler and a Consul and still with room for my A40.

It was Julia who answered my ring. She explained that Geoffrey was out walking.

'In the rain?' I couldn't help asking.

She didn't answer. She looked distraught.

'Tea will be ready in ten minutes,' she said, as she showed me upstairs to my room.

We had tea in the living-room, a spacious room with pale grey walls, deep red carpet, and furnished in elegant — and expensive — simplicity. It took its light from a big oblong window which covered almost the breadth of one wall.

There were two others having tea — a small, wiry man of about fifty in an old tweed suit and yellow tie, and a much younger man, tall, round-shouldered, with a little black beard that didn't quite hide the weakness of his chin.

The bearded one was Philip Brent, Geoffrey's Secretary. The other—whom I had seen, but never spoken to, before—was Owen Stryker, managing director of Harrington and Leigh, who had published all Geoffrey's books.

After the initial civilities Stryker turned to Julia and said: 'Is he not back yet?'

She frowned, then shrugged and replied: 'No. What was it about this time?'

'The usual.' He glanced enquiringly at Julia and, when she nodded, he turned to me and went on:

'Geoffrey and I had a difference of opinion just before he got here. A quarrel, you might call it. He went off in a huff.'

Stryker explained that his firm were bringing out an edition of Geoffrey's diaries and that he was editing them with Geoffrey. Very little progress had been made, for Geoffrey fought every suggested cut.

'The whole idea will have to be scrubbed unless he comes to his senses,' grumbled Stryker. 'You'd almost think he *wanted* to get involved in libel actions.'

'Is there much libellous stuff in the diaries?' I asked.

'God, yes. There are some juicy bits even in the ones he wrote when he was a kid. And he hasn't become any more reticent since.'

'I can remember when he started keeping a diary,' I remarked. 'He'd be about twelve, I think. He used to scribble away in it every night in bed.'

Stryker looked at me with interest.

'Ah! yes,' he said. 'You knew him when he was young. Well, unlike most people, he's kept it up. It's a compulsion with him. Everything that happens to Geoffrey Wallis must be recorded for posterity. There's only one gap: the two years he was abroad after he came down from University.'

'Also the last six months,' Brent amended.

'That's not a gap, Philip. He's still writing it. It's just that he's gone all secretive and won't let us see it.'

Julia was showing signs of impatience. Now she broke in: 'Owen, I wonder if you'd mind—and you too, Philip? There's something I want to discuss with Maurice before Geoffrey gets back.'

Stryker grinned as he got up. 'You don't beat about the bush, Julia, do you?'

Brent followed him out without a word, his face sullen.

Julia began as soon as they were gone. 'Anne's bringing Chris down tonight. We'll have to work fast if we're going to stop this nonsense. She's winning her father round now.'

'Why should we want to stop it?' I asked.

She stared at me. 'Anne's only nineteen, she's far too young to be engaged. Besides, Chris is—well, he's still to make his way in the world.' It was her delicate way of saying that Chris wasn't good enough for her daughter.

I had met Anne only once, when Chris brought her on a surprise visit to me at the University. Like most of Chris's impulsive gestures it hadn't turned out well. Anne was polite to me but not friendly: I guessed that Helen, my ex-wife, had been spinning the tale to her. My impression of Anne was that, far from being too young for Chris, she was much more mature and self-sufficient than he was. I hadn't liked her; but I wasn't prepared to interfere.

'Surely it's up to Chris and Anne. If they've made up their minds, why should we—'

'But she's under age!' Julia exclaimed.

'Well, she'll need her father's consent. But—'

'Her father! She can twist him round her little finger. That's another thing, Maurice. I'm worried about Geoffrey. He's losing his grip.'

I was surprised by Julia's vehemence. And I noticed too the signs of strain, the creases of worry on her brow, the tautness of the skin over her cheekbones. Julia in her youth had just missed being beautiful: her nose was a fraction too long and her lips too thin. But she had always had a striking presence, with her raven hair and tall, slender figure. Today she looked gaunt and haggard.

'What exactly *is* the matter with Geoffrey?' I asked.

Before she could answer we heard a door bang. Julia stiffened in her chair.

A moment later the living-room door was flung open and there stood Geoffrey Wallis, silhouetted in the doorway, water dripping off his raincoat.

'How nice to see you, Maurice. So sorry I wasn't here when you arrived.'

I was shocked. In the eight months since I had seen him he had aged ten years.

CHAPTER 2

Geoffrey Wallis and I had known each other since we were seven. His mother died when he was a baby, and his father was killed in a pit accident not long after they came to Bresford. That would be about 1922.

Sam Wallis, Geoffrey's father, was a big, fresh-faced Scotsman, with a military moustache and a bluff manner. He had come of a good family, Geoffrey always maintained, but a fondness for the bottle had gradually pulled him down the social ladder.

My own father was under-manager of the colliery in which Sam Wallis lost his life. At the inquiry into the accident the system of inspection of equipment in the pit was criticized, and although the report absolved my father from blame, he was sufficiently troubled by his conscience to take the younger boy, Geoffrey, into his family and bring him up as if he were his own son, although he never legally adopted him. His brother, Lionel, was fifteen at the time and already earning his own living. I remember him then as an uncouth, surly youth whom one would never have guessed to be of the same stock as Geoffrey. He stayed with us for a week or two after his father's death and then moved to his uncle's home in Scotland.

From the first Geoffrey and I were rivals rather than friends. Much of it was my fault, I expect. I resented his intrusion into our family and I was jealous of the affection my parents lavished on him. Most of all it enraged me that this newcomer, two months younger than myself, supplanted me in school as the bright boy of the form. We didn't speak of IQs in these days, but Geoffrey's must have been quite exceptionally high. All through our schooldays he had the edge on me, although he didn't work so hard. Only at history, which he found dull, was I his superior; and at games.

It is hard to be objective about someone you dislike. I'm bound to say that most grown-ups found Geoffrey a charming boy, modest, deferential and obliging, with the happy knack of saying what his listener wanted to hear. It is significant, however, that he made no close friends among his schoolfellows. There was an egotism, a self-sufficiency, in him which repelled any close human bond.

We went through grammar school together and then on to University. We started off in Manchester in the same lodgings, but Geoffrey presently moved to rooms where he had more lively company. After that we drifted apart and rarely saw each other except when we returned to Bresford for the vacations.

Geoffrey had already taken to writing, and was displaying the versatility which later puzzled the critics and made him so difficult to classify. A couple of his poems appeared in the *Spectator*, he wrote a short play—an Elizabethan melodrama in blank verse—which was actually produced by the University Dramatic Society, and he had a novel that he was hawking round the publishing houses. (It was published, many years later, by Harrington and Leigh.) I didn't take his writing seriously—clever, undergraduate juggling with words, it seemed to me. It was a fair enough judgement at the time: what I didn't foresee was Geoffrey's potentiality for development.

His literary exercises in no way impaired his University studies, and in due course, in 1936, he got the First in English for which he had clearly been destined. He was offered, and accepted, a post-graduate scholarship to Oxford, and the wind seemed set fair for an academic career of distinction.

But then, in that summer of 1936, Geoffrey took the one unaccountable action of his life. He withdrew his acceptance of the scholarship without explanation and went off to Europe with little money in his pocket and, so far as we could gather, no very definite plans.

We heard nothing from him for a long time, although there was a rumour that he had joined the International Brigade in Spain. Then out of the blue came a postcard from Paris and, a little later, another from Naples. He never explained how he was supporting himself on his Grand Tour. He ended by spending nearly a year in Austria, in a mountain village south of Innsbruck. It was there that he wrote *When The Moon Is Low*, which laid the foundation of his fame.

Geoffrey returned to England in August, 1938, not many weeks before Munich. He walked with a limp but otherwise looked well. I was now doing research in Manchester and, as Geoffrey took lodgings not far from my own, I saw quite a lot of him in the next few months. Having tasted literary success, Geoffrey had now abandoned all thought of an academic career, although I believe he always had lurking regrets. At any rate, his attitude towards my own gradual rise up the University ladder was curiously ambivalent: there was an amused contempt tinged with something like envy.

We were closer, Geoffrey and I, during the year before war broke out than at any time before or since. It was through me that he met Julia. Indeed, it might be said that he prised Julia away from me. That was how Geoffrey regarded it, and perhaps Julia as well; but, truth to tell, I was more than a little relieved when she loosened her grip on me.

I was best man at their wedding in August 1939. It was my last glimpse of Geoffrey and Julia for six years. Within a month I was in the RAF and, after training in Canada, I was shot down behind the German lines in France the following summer. I spent the rest of the war in various prison camps in Germany.

Geoffrey's bad leg exempted him from military service. He was reticent about the injury and would neither confirm nor deny the rumour that he had fought and been wounded in the Spanish Civil War. Indeed, he would never speak at all about the two years he had been abroad.

For me it was a disillusioning experience to get back in the spring of 1945 and meet the wife I had married over five years before and the son, himself now nearly five, whom I had never seen. Helen left me within six months, taking Chris with her. What hurt most was that she had taught Chris to hate me. I gave her a divorce a year or two later.

By contrast the marriage of Geoffrey and Julia flourished. Julia regarded marriage as a social investment and had picked a winner in Geoffrey, whose stock had risen steadily during the war years. He for his part was proud of the aura of 'county' that Julia carried. But there was more to it than that. When Helen and I visited them in the summer of 1945 it was clear to me that Geoffrey at least was genuinely in love with his wife.

That was an unhappy evening, the one Helen and I spent at their house. Geoffrey, whose name in the world of literature was already one to be conjured with, was condescendingly solicitous about my work and about the post I had just accepted in a provincial University. And Julia was no less patronizing. When we got home that night, Helen and I had the first of the quarrels which finally led to her leaving me. She was frankly envious of the material success of Geoffrey and Julia and wondered why I couldn't write 'something that people would want to read instead of that mouldy old history'.

Nettled by that taunt, I rushed into print with my first book before I had put enough work into it. I had the childish desire to prove to Helen that I was as good a historian as Geoffrey was a novelist. It was a fatal blunder. The book was roundly slated as slipshod and immature; and Helen had in any event left me before it appeared. That book was the millstone that held me down ever since. Because of the disastrous impression it had created I still languished, fifteen years later, as a Senior Lecturer in a redbrick University.

In the years since then Geoffrey's path and mine had seldom crossed. But although I disliked Geoffrey and he despised me, we never broke off relations altogether. Having been brought up like brothers in our formative years, we both felt an obligation to remain at least on speaking terms.

Each time I saw Geoffrey, he was a little more prosperous, a little more famous. He had the Midas touch. After a long succession of best-selling novels, he turned to the theatre in 1953 and was at once rewarded with a box-office hit. Then he wrote one or two plays for television, and became so interested in the medium that soon he was appearing regularly himself, in brains trusts and panel games. He was voted TV Personality of 1961 by readers of the *Daily Globe*.

Ever since I had known him Geoffrey had seemed to be protected by a special providence, both in his private and professional life, from the trials that beset lesser mortals. Perhaps he had been cushioned too long against misfortune, so that when it did come, he was no longer equipped to meet it.

Whatever had hit Geoffrey now had hit him hard. The sparkle and vitality had gone out of him. As he chatted to me over a cup of tea, he said the right things, made the right responses, but all in a flat and listless voice. I noticed too that he never addressed himself directly to Julia and avoided her eye.

It was I who sparked off the quarrel.

'Julia tells me Chris is coming down tonight,' I remarked to Geoffrey.

'Yes,' he replied. 'We must have a celebration.'

'A celebration of what?' Julia asked.

'Why, of the engagement, of course.'

Julia flushed. 'But, Geoffrey,' she began, 'you've always—'

'I've changed my mind,' he broke in curtly. 'I gave Anne the all-clear last night. They're getting married in October.'

'Don't you think I might have been consulted first?' said Julia, in a voice dangerously calm.

Geoffrey shrugged with indifference and didn't answer. I got up and left them, making the excuse that I had to unpack. As I went upstairs I could hear Julia's voice raised in anger.

I was as angry as Julia. They had discussed Chris's engagement as though it were no concern of mine.

While I was unpacking, I heard the sound of a car changing gear as it turned in at the gate and, seconds later, as I watched from the window a green Ford Consul emerged from the avenue of shrubs and pulled up outside the porch below me. It was the car I had seen earlier beside the Daimler in the car-port. Anne got out and went into the house.

I met her when I went downstairs a few minutes later.

'I was looking for you, Dr Slater,' she said. 'I'm going in to the station to meet Chris. Would you like to come?'

In looks Anne bore a superficial resemblance to her mother: the same willowy figure, the same dark hair and pale complexion, the same oval face. But her nose was fractionally shorter than Julia's, her lips fuller; and these two insignificant changes in the formula had transformed a striking face into a beautiful one. Besides that, there was an intelligence in Anne's eyes which she had inherited from her father rather than her mother.

She was more friendly today. As we set off down the drive, she referred to our previous meeting.

'Chris shouldn't have been in such a hurry to bring us together,' she said. 'He might have waited till I knew his mother better.'

I recognized this as an apology and an oblique assurance that she no longer believed Helen's slanders about me. No one was taken in by Helen for long. No one except Chris, her son.

'I'm glad you've come,' she added. 'Garston isn't a happy place just now, as you must have seen already. I think you might help.'

'I'm not sure that I'll stay,' I replied, voicing a doubt that had been growing in me ever since I arrived.

Anne stopped the car.

'Please don't say that,' she said earnestly. 'We need your help, Chris and I. Mother's dead set against us getting married. And as for Dad — well, I got his consent last night, but he's quite likely to change round tomorrow. He's so unreliable these days.'

'What is it that's worrying your father, Anne? He looks ill.'

Anne was lighting a cigarette. Glancing at her watch, she remarked:

'Chris's train isn't due for half an hour. I brought you out early so that we could talk. This is as good a place as any.'

We had stopped about a hundred yards short of the village of Gleeve. Just in front of us a rough farm track bisected the road. On the right it climbed leisurely to farm buildings which could just be seen through the misty rain against the skyline; on the left it fell sharply and soon disappeared from view behind a rise in the ground.

Anne was pointing down that track.

'There's a cottage down there behind the hill. You can't see it from the road. Do you know who lives in it? Uncle Lionel.'

'But I thought Lionel lived in Scotland.'

'He did. But he turned up last Christmas and he's been around ever since. We think he's blackmailing Dad.'

It was a strange story Anne told. Lionel Wallis, who had none of his brother's intellectual or literary gifts, had spent his whole working life in his uncle's pharmacy in Cartshaw in Lanarkshire. When his uncle died in the autumn of 1961, Lionel carried on the business for a month or two and then, suddenly, sold out and went south to visit the brother with whom he had had no contact in twenty-five years.

'He arrived unannounced,' Anne said, 'on Christmas Eve. Dad took him into his study and soon we heard them shouting at each other. When Dad came back he told us Uncle Lionel would be staying at Garston for a few days. Actually he was with us five months.'

Lionel's presence had put a strain on the household. Geoffrey had been patient with him, refusing to be goaded by his crude taunts. The others had taken their cue from

Geoffrey, until one day there had been some sort of incident between Lionel and Julia. Lionel had departed within the hour.

'The funny thing is,' said Anne, 'Dad wasn't pleased he was gone. And it was Dad who fixed him up in that cottage down there. He didn't want him too far away.'

'Why?'

Anne hesitated. 'Well, I'm only guessing, but I think Uncle Lionel's applying the screw too tightly and Dad has plans for dealing with him.'

There was a sinister ring about the vague phrase, 'dealing with him.' Geoffrey wasn't one to submit docilely to blackmail.

'What sort of person is Lionel?' I asked.

'Well, he's a drunkard for a start. I've even seen him knocking it back at breakfast. And there's a cruel streak in him. He knows just how to get under Dad's skin and he loves to twist the knife.'

She was silent for so long that I thought she had finished. Then she added, as if to herself: 'Of course, Dad's got other worries too.'

She switched on the ignition and started the engine. We drove through Gleeve and then swung left across the river and round in a semicircle to Minford Junction. We parked in a derelict yard behind the station.

'I always park here,' said Anne. 'There's hardly any space at the front.'

'Do you meet Chris here often?' I asked.

'Every Saturday. I spend the weekends at Garston and Chris joins me on the Saturday as soon as he's off duty. He goes back by the last train.'

Anne worked in the library of one of the London Colleges. She didn't need to take a job, but it gave her a feeling of independence and an excuse for having a flat in London. Besides, she wanted background for the novel she was already writing.

In the distance a train whistled.

'We've got a couple of minutes,' said Anne. 'There's two things I'd be grateful if you'd do, Dr Slater. Try to get Mother to see reason about Chris and me. She's all right really, but she wants me to marry money and class, although I don't give a damn for either. And the other thing is—see what you can do about Dad and Uncle Lionel. I've a feeling something nasty is going to happen if we don't stop it.'

CHAPTER 3

Only two passengers came out by the rear exit—Chris and a florid, portly man in raincoat and bowler hat.

When she saw them, Anne swore under her breath: 'Oh, blast!' she muttered, 'look what he's brought with him!'

The introductions were performed in the rain outside the car. Chris, as he sometimes did, stammered a little over the name. The stranger came to his aid.

'Durrand, dear boy, Durrand. But, as I told you on the train, your father and I are old acquaintances. Fellow alumni of a great University. We—'

'Not *Flash* Durrand!' I interrupted in appalled recognition.

He acknowledged the nickname as if it were a graceful compliment. It was hard to see in this stout, middle-aged man with the hornrimmed spectacles and the pompous manner the Beau Nash of the University of my day.

'I take it you want a lift?' Anne asked him brusquely.

'Well, my dear, that would be nice. My car's in dry dock. But I can easily get a taxi, if—'

'All right, get in. It's raining.'

I was surprised and embarrassed by Anne's rudeness.

So, I felt sure, was Chris. But Durrand himself seemed unaffected. He settled himself comfortably beside me in the back of the car, grunting with satisfaction.

A railway worker going off duty took one of the bicycles that were leaning against a wall of the yard and cycled past our car and down the road. After a few yards he turned sharp right and disappeared from view.

'Wonder when they'll repair that bridge,' Durrand remarked.

As we passed the intersection in the car a moment later, I looked down the lane that the cyclist had taken. It soon dipped out of view into the valley, but reappeared on the other side and climbed past an isolated white cottage. Beyond, and further to the left, I could see the spire of Gleeve church.

'Is that a short cut to Gleeve?' I asked.

'It would be,' said Anne, 'if the bridge were still there. It's only two miles that way, instead of six by the main road. But the bridge was swept away in the floods last November. There's just a ford now.'

I was getting my bearings.

'That'll be where Lionel Wallis lives?' I asked, pointing to the cottage I had seen.

'Yes,' said Durrand. But he had tired of the subject; he wanted to tell me about himself. I learned that he was a partner in a legal firm in the City, that he was a widower, and that he had bought a house in Gleeve two years before.

Remembering that Geoffrey and he had once been friends, I asked Durrand if he had chosen Gleeve so as to be near the Wallises. There was a suppressed snort from Anne in the front seat. Durrand seemed to find the question hard to answer. Finally he said, picking his words carefully as though he were giving evidence in a court of law:

'I am Geoffrey's lawyer, but one doesn't see him socially

nowadays as much as one would like.'

We dropped Durrand at a small, red-roofed bungalow opposite Gleeve Post Office. He made me promise to call round for a drink the following evening.

'That man gives me the creeps,' Anne remarked, as we drove off.

'Don't you think you're too hard on him, darling?' said Chris. 'I know he's a bore, but—'

'Take it from me, Chris, Durrand is poison. I know.' She was very emphatic.

Chris didn't answer. Although I couldn't see his face, I knew exactly the expression of unconvinced obstinacy it would be wearing.

People were apt to misjudge Chris. He looked so strong and confident that they never guessed the struggle he had to keep up the facade. He liked to see things in clear blacks and whites and distrusted the greys. That was what had vitiated his relationship with me. Having been brought up by his mother in the creed that I was a monster of depravity, he found that view of me impossible to maintain as he got to know me better. Perhaps if I had told him frankly the full story of my marriage, I might have won him over completely. But I couldn't bring myself to do it, for Chris meant so much to Helen. So I never criticized his mother to him, beyond occasionally hinting that there had been faults on both sides. That wasn't what Chris wanted at all: for him there had to be a right and a wrong, a good and a bad, and he was uneasy with me because of his uncertainty on which side of the line I stood.

The anti-intellectual bias that Helen had instilled into Chris also put me at a disadvantage. I had always to avoid even the appearance of talking down to him or of disparaging his intelligence or education, for he was quick to take offence. Actually he had above-average intelligence and he did well at school. But he was determined not to be a pen-pusher, as he contemptuously labelled every profession from university teacher to civil service clerk. So, after doing his National Service, he was now training in hotel management. It was an odd choice of career, but he seemed to enjoy it.

Considering his home circumstances and upbringing Chris had turned out well, and I was proud of him. But I feared for him too. Behind his solid, phlegmatic appearance he was vulnerable and easily hurt. What Chris needed above all was to meet and to marry a girl who would give him the love and understanding and stability that he had never had at home.

I wondered whether Anne could fill that role. I wished I knew her better. I watched them as they got out of the car at Garston, Chris tall, fair, broad-shouldered and suntanned, Anne slim, dark and pale-complexioned. Anne tucked her fiancé's arm in hers as they walked, smiling, into the house.

CHAPTER 4

I sometimes ask myself whether I shouldn't have foreseen and prevented the tragedy. Certainly, as I look back now on my first week at Garston, I can see clearly the omens of what was impending. But without the benefits of hindsight it was impossible to interpret the signs, to eliminate the irrelevancies and to discern the malignant pattern running through events.

I was enjoying my holiday. My second book—a life of Warren Hastings—had been completed a couple of months previously and was now in the press. I was still basking in the release from nearly eight years' solid work, and although I had brought to Garston reference books and notes for an article I had been asked to write, they remained in a suitcase in my room.

Geoffrey made intermittent efforts to be hospitable and there were times when he seemed almost himself again. But always there was that abstracted look in his eyes.

He was given to bursts of temper, too. At dinner on that first Saturday night he suddenly flared up when Chris unwisely disparaged television panel games as adolescent and trivial. It was a tactless remark, considering that Geoffrey himself regularly took part in them. All the same, his reaction was disproportionately violent. Chris reddened, and the look he gave Geoffrey told me how much he disliked him.

Strangely enough, Chris got on better with Julia. She made no bones about her opinion that Chris would not make an acceptable son-in-law; but she was prepared to like him as a person.

Chris returned to London by the last train on the Saturday night. And the following afternoon Geoffrey departed in his Daimler. He was to appear on television in the evening and would spend the night at his Club, he told us.

The whole atmosphere at Garston lightened as soon as Geoffrey had gone. Even Anne, who had emerged pale and anxious from a long session with her father in his study earlier in the day, visibly relaxed. She told me that Geoffrey was hedging again and threatening to withdraw his consent to the marriage.

Durrand telephoned to remind me of his invitation and to ask if Mrs Wallis and her daughter would care to join me. He had seen Geoffrey's Daimler pass, apparently, and knew he was away. Julia accepted with alacrity; Anne smiled sardonically and said no.

Julia and I were the only guests. The house was a small one, but exquisitely furnished. The walls of the room he showed us into proclaimed his interest in contemporary art.

At university Durrand had been something of a dandy. He still dressed well, I noticed, but not so ostentatiously as in the past. His grey suit was immaculately cut and bore the hallmark of Savile Row.

We talked about politics. Although Durrand had been a socialist in his younger days, I wasn't surprised to find that he had put these indiscretions behind him. He now described himself as a left-wing Tory, whatever that meant.

He was waxing indignant over the anti-nuclear demonstrations.

'I've no patience with these people,' he said. 'They're just playing the Russians' game for them. Of course,' he added, 'they're riddled with communists.'

When I mildly remonstrated, his answer was to quote a specific example.

'Look at Stryker,' he said. 'He's one of the ringleaders. And he's a party member.'

'Owen Stryker?' said Julia, showing interest. 'You say he's a communist?'

'Good heavens! it's common knowledge. I'm surprised your husband sees so much of him.'

'Only in the way of business,' Julia replied. But I could see that she was pondering what difference this information ought to make in her attitude to Stryker. She was always concerned about the social niceties.

'Incidentally,' Durrand went on, 'one wonders what common interest Stryker has with your brother-in-law.'

Julia's attention was really roused now.

'What do you mean?' she asked sharply.

'Well, Stryker is down at the cottage every other day.'

'Why didn't you—' she began, and then broke off as she caught a warning look from Durrand. I intercepted it too, a light pursing of the lips and a swift glance towards me.

It was illuminating. Julia had been about to say 'Why

didn't you tell me?' as if surprised that he should have withheld anything from her. And Durrand had tried to stop her from letting me see that they were on such close terms. I was beginning to suspect why Durrand had bought a house in Gleeve, and why Anne disliked him so much. It was significant, too, that the invitation to Julia today had been deferred until Geoffrey was safely on his way to London.

Durrand filled in as if nothing untoward had happened. His technique was so slick that I wondered if I had imagined the incident.

'To tell you the truth,' he said, turning to me, 'I'm sorry I ever let that cottage to Lionel Wallis. I only did it as a favour to Geoffrey. Lionel's made a slum of it. And he hasn't done a hand's turn in the garden.'

'Is it your cottage?' I asked in surprise.

'Well, no. But I've got the handling of it. The owner's abroad. Look here,' he added with concern, 'your glass is empty. This will never do.' And when he had done his duty as host, he piloted the conversation into safer channels.

Geoffrey didn't appear at Garston again until the Wednesday. Although Julia had expected him back sooner, she wasn't worried by his absence. This sort of thing happened regularly, I gathered.

Julia herself I scarcely saw except at meals. She muttered something about domestic chores, but otherwise made no apology for leaving me to my own devices. I might, perhaps, have taken offence, especially with Geoffrey, for this neglect, but it suited me well enough to laze around on my own.

The weather had improved. It was hot enough on the Monday afternoon for me to lounge on a deck chair on the terrace and read a novel. It was one of Geoffrey's— *The Rebel*. Not his best, perhaps, but the technique, as always, was flawless. I had my own views of Geoffrey as a creative artist, but I had to admit that as a craftsman he was unsurpassed.

Midway through the afternoon I was interrupted by Philip Brent, Geoffrey's secretary. My earlier attempts to be friendly had been rebuffed, but now he seemed anxious to make amends. He brought over a glass of lime juice and sat on the grass beside my chair while I drank it.

Although Philip Brent had a leading part to play in the drama that was unfolding, I find him hardest of all the characters to give flesh and bone to. He was odd in appearance, with his large head and unruly hair and carefully tended beard. When he spoke in that squeaky voice with the hint of a foreign accent, you felt you had strayed into amateur theatricals.

He was easier to understand when you knew his background, of which I had heard something from Julia. According to her, Brent was half Italian. His father had died before he was born and his mother had taken him back to Italy, where he lived till he was twelve. Then he had been sent to England to be educated at the minor public school which his father had attended. Philip went on to Cambridge, where he read Languages and scraped a lower second in the Tripos. He wanted to write, but his background was all against him. He had become more English than the English and his stuff read like vintage Kipling. After a year or so of bombarding the publishers and magazine editors, he had been glad to take a job as Geoffrey Wallis's secretary.

I asked Brent now how he had got the job.

'It was through my tutor at Pembroke. Mr Wallis knew him.'

'You like working for Geoffrey?'

'Oh! yes . . . Or, at least I did.'

He didn't need much prompting after that.

'I wish I knew what was wrong with him,' he said plaintively. 'He's hardly written a line for months.'

Until recently Geoffrey had been, as I would have expected, the most methodical of writers. He would dictate into his tape-recorder for a couple of hours in the morning and an hour after lunch. Then between tea and dinner he would revise Brent's typescript of the previous day's output. He rarely fell short of his daily target of 2,500 words and, as he worked a six-day week (only Saturday was a *dies non*), it wasn't surprising that he was so prolific. However, a few months ago the machine had suddenly ground to a halt. Geoffrey had been working on a play and had completed the second act by the middle of February. Now, five months later, he still hadn't got any further with it.

'Was it Lionel's arrival that upset him?' I asked.

'Oh! no. When his brother came to Garston last Christmas, Mr. Wallis was angry, but it didn't really put him off his stride. No, this depression came on more than a month later.'

'Any idea what caused it?'

Brent hesitated. 'I think it had something to do with Mrs Wallis,' he said, with a knowing smile. I hastily changed the subject by asking what he thought of Lionel.

He didn't like him. No one seemed to have a good word for Lionel. They all complained of his drunkenness and his surliness. Brent had an additional charge: he wasn't a gentleman.

'All the same,' he added, 'I wouldn't like him to come to any harm.'

'What do you mean?'

'I'm afraid Mr Wallis is planning to murder his brother.'

It all came pouring out then. Brent, like Anne, believed that Lionel was blackmailing Geoffrey, and—again like her—he believed that Geoffrey wasn't going to take it lying down. But in Brent's estimation the only effective way to deal with a blackmailer was to kill him and that was exactly what Geoffrey was planning to do.

The evidence on which he founded these suspicions was ludicrously tenuous. Geoffrey had remarked to Brent recently that he had a 'certain little local difficulty' to attend to, and the context had made it plain that the little local difficulty was Lionel. Geoffrey had been cleaning his revolver at the time, and that was enough to convince Brent that Lionel's life was in danger.

It was hard not to smile. He sensed my derision.

'It may sound silly,' he said huffily, 'but if you'd seen his face . . .'

It was easy to shrug off Brent's premonitions. But Owen Stryker was another matter.

He turned up at Garston on the Tuesday morning, intending to continue work with Geoffrey on the diaries. When he learned that Geoffrey wasn't back from London, he was furious.

'There's no excuse,' he said. 'He knew I was coming this morning.'

'Can't you get on without him?' I asked.

'He keeps the damned diaries locked up and hides the key.'

By the time Julia brought us coffee, Stryker had cooled down a little.

'What's got into your husband, Julia?' he remarked. 'He never used to behave like this.'

Julia made a vague reply and soon left us.

Stryker grinned. '*She* knows what's wrong,' he said, 'but she won't say. She's frightened.'

'Frightened of what?'

'Frightened of Geoffrey. Frightened of what he's going to do.'

'And what *is* he going to do?'

Stryker had taken a pipe from his pocket and was filling

it while he eyed me as if weighing up how much he could
tell me.

'Well, Professor,' he said at last, 'I'd only be guessing.
But you'll soon find out for yourself. It's planned for this
weekend. Geoffrey's made that clear.'

'Brent believes he's going to murder Lionel,' I said,
hoping to startle him.

The lighted match paused momentarily on its way to
the bowl of the pipe.

'Does he now?' he said mildly.

After a moment he added: 'Would you like to meet
Lionel?'

'Now?'

'Why not? My morning's wasted anyway. Besides, it's
the best time to call on Lionel. He should still be sober.'

We walked down to the village. Stryker took me by the
back way, through a gate behind the tennis court and
along a grassy path which joined a farm road after a
couple of hundred yards.

'This is a short cut,' said Stryker. 'Very secluded. Julia
uses it a lot.'

He threw the remark over his shoulder as he strode out
vigorously ahead of me. To make sure that I took his
meaning, he went on:

'You can get to Arthur Durrand's house this way without going through the village at all. See, there's the path.'
He pointed to a track veering off to the right.

A little further on the farm road itself debouched on
the main road. I recognized where we were. It was the
crossroads just on the Garston side of Gleeve. Across the
main road from us was the track leading down to Lionel's
cottage.

Stryker continued to talk to me in short staccato bursts.
He was a cocksure little man, with no inhibitions about
gossiping to strangers.

'Can't think what she sees in that man,' he said. 'Mind

you, I never blame a woman for kicking over the traces. But why Durrand? Julia's a handsome filly. She could have done better for herself than that.'

We were approaching the cottage now. Hidden from the road above, it nestled picturesquely against the hillside, with whitewashed walls and red-tiled roof. The track we had been following continued past the cottage and down to the stream that ran through the village. This was where the bridge had been: some of the metal stanchions were still in position. On the other side the road climbed the hill and disappeared towards Minford.

A few yards upstream a series of large flat stones formed a ford across the water. A couple of girls were sitting on one of the stones, trailing their legs in the water. A small tent was pitched nearby.

We went through the wicket gate into the overgrown garden and knocked at the door of the cottage. The room Lionel took us into was sparsely furnished: a couple of easy chairs and some small chairs, a table with a television set on it, a shelf lined with books; that was about all. But the room was clean and tidy and there was none of the squalor at which Durrand had hinted.

Lionel himself was a surprise. I had imagined him as a big man, no doubt because he had seemed enormous when I was seven and he was fifteen. In fact he was under average height, perhaps a little smaller than Geoffrey, whom he closely resembled. He was sprucely dressed in grey cardigan, sports shirt and slacks and there were few of the signs I would have expected in a man reputed to be an alcoholic.

All the same he did at once offer us a drink and, although both Stryker and I declined, he poured himself a stiff whisky. He took it neat.

'You're Chris's father?' he said to me. 'A fine boy.'

He spoke with a Scottish accent and with the ingratiating manner of a shopkeeper addressing an important customer.

We chatted about Chris and Anne, for whom Lionel professed to have a warm regard. Then Stryker asked Lionel if he had seen his brother recently.

Just for a moment I saw naked emotion in Lionel's eyes — hatred, fear, perhaps a mixture of both. But when he answered, his voice was mild and servile as before.

'No,' he said. 'I don't see much of Geoff these days. Of course, we haven't a great deal in common.' And he smiled apologetically. I saw his eye straying towards the bottle on the table.

We left soon afterwards.

'What do you make of him?' asked Stryker, as we toiled back up the track.

'Rather pathetic,' I replied. 'Is he really blackmailing Geoffrey?'

'Not much doubt about it. Geoffrey would never have given him house-room for five months if Lionel didn't have some hold over him. Besides, why has he settled in that godawful cottage? He's not there for his health.'

After a moment he added: 'In a way it's a pity he was sober when you met him. He's better company when he's tight.'

'How did you get to know him?'

'I used to meet him up at Garston when he was staying there. I discovered he has the same hobby as I have — stamp-collecting. After he moved down to the cottage I started dropping in occasionally on my way home from Garston. I usually take him a few stamps. I'm sorry for him.'

I wondered if that was his only reason for befriending Lionel. Stryker didn't seem to me the kind of person who would waste much time on pity.

CHAPTER 5

When Geoffrey returned about midday on Wednesday it seemed at first that he had recovered his spirits. He apologized for neglecting his guest and by way of atonement he had me on the tennis court that afternoon in the broiling sun.

There was, however, a feverishness in his gaiety. One felt it wouldn't last. At tea Julia, taking advantage of her husband's good humour, told him that Jane, their younger daughter, who was due home from school on Friday evening, had phoned to ask if she could spend the first week of her holiday with a school friend.

'I said it would be all right,' said Julia. 'She'll be here on Friday to unpack and she'll leave again on Saturday morning.'

Geoffrey exploded. 'You had no right to agree to that. I told you I wanted the whole family here this weekend.'

'Why?' Julia's tone was angry and apprehensive at the same time.

'Never mind why. Just get on that phone and tell Jane she's not going.'

'If that's what you want, you can phone yourself,' Julia snapped.

'Very well, I will.' And he stormed out of the room and slammed the door behind him.

Julia sighed in exasperation. But on Philip Brent's face I detected a look of malicious pleasure. He had enjoyed the quarrel.

Later that evening I wanted to use the telephone myself. I lifted the phone in the hall, but replaced it when I heard voices from the earpiece. Geoffrey was phoning from the extension in his study.

I caught a snatch of conversation. First Geoffrey: '—see you before dinner.' And then the reply: 'All right, make it 6.15. Be sure—'

The second voice was familiar, but it was some time before I could place it. It was the voice of Lionel Wallis.

I spent most of Thursday with Geoffrey. It was the only time all that week that I had a real chance to talk to him. Perhaps I should have made better use of it; perhaps if I had been more pressing, he would have told me what was on his mind, what he was planning to do.

He did drop some hints. I remember, for example, his odd reply when I asked him why he was doing no writing.

'One can't write in the shadow of great events. One waits until the dust has settled.'

'And when is that likely to be?'

'Soon. Just bear with us for another few days, Maurice, and it'll all be clear to you.' When I mentioned my meeting with Lionel, he frowned.

'He's a bastard, Maurice, a proper bastard. If I told you what he's—but he won't trouble me much longer.'

'Why not?'

A cunning look came over his face.

'I've got my plans,' he said.

He talked about his diary.

'It's no literary masterpiece,' he said, 'but it'll cause a stir all the same. I've always intended it to be published—I wasn't just writing for fun. I used to think it had better wait till after I'm dead. But that way I would miss all the fun. Some people aren't going to like it, you know.'

'What about libel?'

He snorted.

'Not much fear of that when Owen Stryker's using the red pencil. He's as timid as a kitten. Inquisitive, too,' he added reflectively. 'I've told him we're not using the latest diaries. Yet he keeps trying to get hold of them. I sometimes wonder . . .'

He didn't finish the sentence.

We sat in the garden most of the morning. After lunch Geoffrey took me for a run in the Daimler. We kept to minor roads most of the time and I doubt if Geoffrey consciously chose any particular route. My guess is that the act of driving was a kind of tranquillizer for him.

He spoke from time to time about his family. Of Julia he said little, but the hardness of his tone (and, indeed, his whole manner to her ever since I had come to Garston) expressed more eloquently than words his feelings towards her.

It was his two daughters he seemed to be concerned about.

'Of course, Anne can stand on her own feet—she's as tough as I am. And anyway she's got Chris. But this'll be a shock for Jane.'

'You're talking in riddles, Geoffrey. What are you planning to do? Commit a murder?'

Although I asked the question jocularly, I was sufficiently uneasy at Geoffrey's strange manner to be reminded of what Brent had said.

His answer was another riddle:

'I did consider that. But I took advice and—well, I've got a better plan now. It's only a side issue anyway.'

He refused to be more specific.

One other snippet of conversation I remember. Geoffrey asked me what I thought of his secretary, Philip Brent. Although I tried to be fair in my reply, he quickly sensed that I disapproved of Brent and broke in sharply:

'Don't underestimate Philip. He's intelligent. Also, he's *loyal*, which is rare enough these days.' There was bitterness in his voice.

When we got back from our drive, Julia was speaking on the telephone in the hall. She looked flustered when she saw us and hurriedly rang off.

Geoffrey was quick to draw the obvious conclusion.

'How *is* Arthur?' he asked her with a sour smile.

Julia flushed and didn't answer. She had handled the situation so clumsily that I almost suspected her of deliberately drawing attention to her phone call to Durrand.

Friday was a quiet day. Geoffrey went off to London in the forenoon and returned after tea. He retired to his study and we didn't see him again, except at dinner, when he was preoccupied and uncommunicative.

Anne arrived home for the weekend about six o'clock. She brought with her her sister, whom she had collected from her school earlier in the afternoon.

I hadn't met Jane before. She had just turned sixteen and was pretty in a teenage fashion, with pony-tail, pale face and sulky, pouting lips.

Perhaps the pout wasn't a permanent feature, for at the moment she was thoroughly disgruntled by the cancellation of her holiday with her school friend. Her way of expressing her displeasure was to create as much noise as she could. Banging doors followed her progress through the house. As soon as she was out of her school uniform and into a black sweater and jeans, she put on a record-player at full blast in the living-room while she contorted herself in the movements of the twist.

A disagreeable child. So at least it seemed to me at first. But when she talked to me after dinner, something of her loneliness got through to me.

We had had a set of tennis, Anne and I against Philip Brent and Jane. Afterwards Philip and Anne went indoors. Jane stretched herself out on the bank beside the court and began moodily to chew a blade of grass. I sat down beside her.

'Why is life so hellish?' Jane asked, with a quick glance

to see if I was shocked by the adjective.

'You mean, because you're not getting your holiday?'

She shook her head impatiently.

'It's not just that. It's no fun coming home nowadays. Daddy and Mummy have no time for me.'

'I'm sure you're imagining that,' I said, but without conviction. She didn't answer.

After a bit she said: 'Something's cooking. Anne's got the jitters too, and if *she's* het up it must be bad.

'I wish I was clever like Anne,' she added wistfully. 'And beautiful too. Plain Jane, that's me.'

There were tears in her eyes.

'How do you like Chris?' I asked, trying to divert her.

Her eyes lit up: her face was transformed.

'Oh! he's the most!'

Then the lips pouted again. 'But Anne's got him too. It's not fair.'

CHAPTER 6

When I was questioned later about that Saturday, I found it was the little, irrelevant details that were etched indelibly in my mind: the scratch on Geoffrey's face where he had cut himself shaving; Julia's irritation at lunch that the joint was overdone; the bright red varnish on Jane's nails which she was promptly made to remove; the drone of the motor-mower; Philip Brent's elegant college blazer.

And the heat. The hottest spell since August 1953, the papers were saying. It was a sultry, enervating heat, with a threat of thunder.

After lunch I took refuge in the comparative coolness of the library and dozed over a book. Julia came in at half past four with tea on a tray. She was so pale and haggard that I asked her if she was feeling all right.

'I've got a headache,' she replied. 'It's the weather. I'm going upstairs to lie down for a bit.'

I wrote one or two letters after tea. Then I must have dozed off again. When I wakened, stiff and uncomfortable, it was 6.25 on the clock on the mantelshelf.

I wandered out into the hall. As soon as I opened the library door I could hear the strains of music from the direction of the living-room. Jane must have the record-player on again.

Anne was just going out of the front door.

'I'm off to meet Chris,' she said.

'Where is everybody?' I asked her.

'Well, Dad left a while ago to go up to town. Mother's lying down, I think. Jane—well, you can hear Jane. And I haven't seen Philip all afternoon.'

Anne went out, and I heard her car start up and move off. I was glad she hadn't invited me to go with her this week. I wanted to soak in a hot bath to get rid of my stiffness.

But first I looked into the living-room to have a word with Jane. She wasn't there, although an LP was still blaring on the record-player. Then I glanced out of the window and saw her lying on the grass, propped on her elbows and munching a banana. I turned off the record and went out and joined her.

She had a transistor radio beside her and was listening to a commentary on one of the county matches.

'Are you interested in cricket?' I asked in surprise.

She nodded. 'We play it at school. I root for Surrey. But this is dreary stuff.' She turned down the sound.

'That horrid little man was here this afternoon,' she said unexpectedly, 'you know, the red-faced one that smokes cigars.'

'Stryker?'

'Yes, Daddy's publisher. Ugh! He's nauseating.'

'What's wrong with him?'

'It's the way he looks at me. You know, like he was taking my clothes off. And it's worse for Anne. He's really gone on her.'

'You're imagining it,' I said.

'I'm not!' she replied indignantly. 'You ask Anne. Anyway, he got an earful from Daddy today.'

She told me that Stryker had arrived about three o'clock. After half an hour with Geoffrey in his study they had come out together, talking angrily. Stryker had jumped into his car and driven off 'with a flea in his ear', to use Jane's phrase.

We talked for a few minutes longer, but Jane's eyes were straying towards the radio. I got up and walked back to the house. The scent of new-mown grass mingled with the cloying perfume of the roses. Everything was very still. From behind me the voice of the commentator took up its tale: '. . . the final over of the day, and it's going to be bowled by . . .' He sounded drowsy too.

Dinner was late. And it was an uncomfortable meal, with everybody irritable and snappish. The weather, I suppose, had something to do with it, but the absence of Geoffrey heightened the tension. We all knew he had something planned for that weekend and we were waiting for it to break.

Worst of all was Chris, who flew off the handle at a rather condescending remark by Philip Brent which he chose to regard as a sneer at his lack of education.

I admired Anne's diplomacy. While appearing to take Chris's side, she contrived to make an unspoken appeal to Brent. Brent gallantly apologized, and the incident was over.

But Chris still looked resentful and I realised that something more than Brent's tactlessness had upset him. After the meal I sought him out and asked what had happened. The cold, appraising look he gave me was a bleak reminder of days I had thought were past. He turned my questions aside; I couldn't get through to him. Presently he went off with Anne and I didn't see him again that night.

I went to bed early but I couldn't sleep. Even with the windows wide open the room was airless and stuffy.

I heard Anne drive off with Chris to get the last train at Minford. Some time later there was the hum from the engine of a car climbing the drive, then lights flashed across the bedroom wall as it turned to the car-port. A door slammed, and light footsteps crossed the gravel below my window. Then I heard voices.

'Heavens, Mother, what a fright you gave me! What are you doing out here?'

Then Julia's voice: 'Oh! it's you, Anne. When I heard the car, I thought it might be your father.'

'Is he not back yet?'

'No. And I can't think why—'

'He'll be at his Club. He often—'

'Anne, I'm frightened. I looked in his desk just now and his revolver's gone.'

I couldn't catch any more as the footsteps receded towards the front door. Just then there was the first rumble of thunder.

After the storm Sunday morning dawned cool and tranquil. Although light rain was still falling when I got up, a break in the clouds to the east promised better things. The bird chorus was shriller and more cheerful this morning.

The change in the weather had done nothing for Julia. Her face was ashen, as if she hadn't slept.

However, she was calm enough. At breakfast Philip Brent asked when Geoffrey would be back.

'He stayed in town overnight,' Julia replied. 'He won't

be home now till after his show this evening.'

I supposed she must have phoned Geoffrey at his Club. She no longer seemed anxious about his absence.

The day dragged on interminably. Jane did some telephoning and presently a self-conscious, pimply youth, about her own age, arrived on a motorcycle and bore her proudly off, Julia looking on with abstracted disapproval. The rest of us browsed over the Sunday papers.

After tea I shook off my lethargy and went for a walk. When I got back, Arthur Durrand was getting out of his car. Geoffrey had invited him for dinner, he explained to me.

'Geoffrey did?' I couldn't hide my surprise.

'Changed days, eh? Frankly, old man, I thought it was all washed up between Geoffrey and me. But I got this note on Friday. Very formal. Said he'd an important matter to discuss with his family on Sunday evening and he'd like me, as his lawyer, to be present. Perhaps I would care to have dinner first.'

'But Geoffrey's in London.'

'Well, he didn't actually say *he* would be dining here. He'll be back as soon as his show's over, no doubt.'

Julia was expecting Durrand and had drinks ready. No one mentioned the reason for his visit although it was uppermost in our minds. We made a laboured pretence of light conversation. But there were uneasy pauses.

About ten to seven the telephone rang. Anne went out to answer it. She came back a moment later, looking puzzled.

'It's the BBC,' she said. 'They want to know where Dad is. He should have been there at 6.30 for a run through of tonight's performance. You'd better speak to them, Mother.'

Julia was away for a long time.

When she came back, she said: 'I've been phoning Geoffrey's Club. He wasn't there last night.'

'But, Mother,' said Anne, 'I thought you phoned this morning.'

'No, I—I—' Julia broke off. She was deathly white and swayed a little on her feet.

I helped her to a chair.

'Get some brandy,' I said to Philip Brent. But Anne had already gone out for it.

When Julia had recovered, somebody suggested phoning the police, but no one made any move to do it.

'When does his programme come on?' I asked.

'7.15,' said Brent, and switched on the television set.

We sat in silence while the previous programme ended. 'And now,' said the announcer, 'it's time for another edition of . . . There is a change in tonight's panel from that published in the *Radio Times*. Owing to a sudden indisposition, Geoffrey Wallis is unable to be with us. His place is being taken, at very short notice, by that popular . . .'

Brent switched off.

'There's something wrong,' he said. 'Mr Wallis never misses appointments.'

'When did Geoffrey leave here yesterday?' Julia asked suddenly.

'About ten past six,' said Anne. 'He said he was going up to town. He didn't say when he would be back.'

Then I remembered.

'I heard Geoffrey make an appointment with his brother for 6.15,' I said. 'I don't know what night it was for, but it could have been yesterday. Perhaps that's where he was making for when he left here.'

My remark was received in silence.

'Well,' I added, 'shouldn't we at least phone Lionel and ask if he's seen Geoffrey?'

'No,' said Julia quickly. 'Geoffrey would never go there. He and Lionel weren't speaking.'

'They were speaking on the phone the other night,' I

reiterated, nettled at her obstinacy. 'There can be no harm in asking.'

Julia shrugged. 'Please yourself,' she said ungraciously.

Durrand gave me the number. I went out to the hall and dialled it. There was no reply.

'I'm going down there,' I said. 'Is anyone coming?'

Again there was silence. Then Anne spoke:

'I'll come,' she said.

As we drove to the village Anne remarked:

'Mother has a thing about Uncle Lionel. She won't allow his name to be mentioned since — well, there was an incident, you know.'

'So I've heard.'

We reached the crossroads and turned down towards Lionel's cottage. Last night's downpour had left the road wet and greasy, and even in bottom gear the wheels were skidding on the steep hill.

I stopped beside the cottage. The first thing I noticed was a milk bottle and the *Sunday Telegraph* outside the gate.

'Look,' said Anne, pointing at the ground in front of us. 'There's been a car here. See the tyre-marks.'

'How did it get out? There were no tracks on the road we've just come down.'

'It must have gone the other way. You can get round the back of the cottage and along by the river and come out at the other end of the village.'

We got out and walked forward to have a closer look. Anne was right. The tracks led down towards the river, then turned right, behind the cottage, in the direction of Gleeve.

'Dr Slater!'

The urgency in Anne's voice made me turn sharply.

'Yes?'

'What time did the rain start last night?'

'About half past eleven. Why?'

'Well, the ground was bone-hard until then. So this car must have left here after the rain started. Quite a bit after.'

'What of it?'

'That's Dad's Daimler. I'm sure that's the tread. So Dad must have been here at midnight or later last night. I don't like this.'

We went through the gate and up to the cottage and tried the door. It was locked.

I moved round to a window and peered in. It was the room into which Lionel had taken Stryker and me a day or two before.

'Anne,' I said, 'we'll have to get the police. There's been a hell of a fight in here.'

'Is there — can you see — ?' Anne was on the verge of breaking down.

'No,' I said, 'I can't see anyone. Just the furniture all smashed about and a broken bottle on the floor.'

As Gleeve's one policeman was on holiday that weekend, we had to contact the Minford police station. They sent along a sergeant and a constable.

There was a maddening delay while Sergeant Wain, a stickler for the regulations, considered whether the circumstances warranted breaking into the cottage. Meanwhile I had phoned Garston from the village to let them know what was going on, and presently Durrand arrived with Philip Brent.

'Julia wanted to come too,' he said, 'but I made her stay with Jane.'

I remembered that it was Durrand who had let the cottage to Lionel.

'Have you a key?' I asked him.

'Not here. It's in my office in London.'

However, Sergeant Wain had now reached a decision.

Having found the door and all the windows locked, he smashed the kitchen window, put his hand in to release the catch, and opened the window. The young constable climbed in and opened the front door. We followed the sergeant in, ignoring his half-hearted protest.

A smell of spirits assailed us. I was immediately behind the sergeant, who had stopped at the open door of the sitting-room and was gazing in.

The room had been wrecked. The table was upended, and the television set lay on the floor beside it, its screen shattered; two of the small wooden chairs had been broken; the mirror over the fireplace was smashed. A broken bottle of whisky lay half under one of the arm-chairs, and nearby, on its side but unbroken, a siphon of soda. Two glasses, also unbroken, stood on the mantel-shelf.

All this I took in at first glance. Then the central feature got through to me — the enormous, dark red stain on the green rug by the fire, and numerous smaller rustlike patches on the linoleum that covered the rest of the room. The sergeant saw it at the same moment.

'God!' he said, with awe in his voice, 'there's been murder done here.'

Anne, who was behind me, trying to peer over my shoulder, caught the word 'murder'.

'Is it — is — ' Her voice tailed off. I looked round sharply as she crumpled. Brent caught her before she fell and helped me carry her outside.

The sergeant meanwhile had a rapid look round the rest of the cottage. He was asserting his authority with more confidence, now that he was satisfied that his forcible entry was justified. He ordered us all outside and told the constable to stand guard while he went to the village to phone for his Inspector.

'There's a telephone in the cottage,' Durrand pointed out.

'Ah! yes, sir, but we got to think about fingerprints.
Can't be too careful in these cases, I always say.'

Anne quickly came round. I helped her to my car.

'Sorry,' she said, smiling wanly. 'I've never done that
before. It was the thought that Dad—'

'Leave it just now, Anne. We don't know yet what's
happened.'

'Oh! yes, we do. Dad has killed Uncle Lionel. That's
what he's been planning all these weeks.'

CHAPTER 7

Julia showed remarkable resilience. She had a curious
logic which assured her that it was better to know the
worst had happened than to be afraid it was going to.
Besides, she took comfort from the evidence of a struggle:
that proved, she said, that Geoffrey had killed in self-
defence.

The police were in no doubt that Lionel was dead,
although his body hadn't been found. Their surgeon was
emphatic that no one could have lost so much blood and
lived. They had also recovered a couple of bullets from a
.38, one embedded in the wall of the sitting-room and
one lying in the hearth.

Apart from Jane, who had been bundled off early,
none of us got to bed that night. It was close on midnight
before the inspector was through questioning us, and
after that it seemed better to sit up and wait. But no news
came.

Arthur Durrand departed after breakfast. I wanted to
leave too, but Julia asked me to stay and help Brent in
holding the press at bay.

One or two of the morning papers had a paragraph
about Geoffrey's last-minute withdrawal from the tele-

vision show. But it wasn't till nearly ten o'clock that the press got wind of what was going on. After that we were besieged. A promising enough story in its own right, with Geoffrey Wallis involved it was heady stuff. For Geoffrey was news; and Geoffrey as a suspected murderer was sensation.

After the first hour we put the telephone off the hook and refused to answer the doorbell. But when Julia saw a group of newspapermen swarming round the gardener, she decided it would be better if Brent and I gave them a statement.

Brent did most of the talking. The clicking of the cameras and the rapid-fire questions seemed to loosen his tongue and soon he was giving them a vivid description of the blood and devastation in Lionel's cottage. Before I could stop him he went on to say that Geoffrey had killed his brother 'either accidentally or in self-defence.'

His indiscretion did little harm, because the papers couldn't print it anyway, although they did manage pretty skilfully to get it across to their readers, without actually saying so, that Geoffrey Wallis was wanted for the murder of his brother.

Soon there were developments in what the press was calling 'the nationwide hunt for Geoffrey Wallis'. An attendant at an all-night garage in north London remembered the Daimler coming in for a fill-up at 3 a.m. on the Sunday. Geoffrey had been driving and appeared to be alone in the car. He had next been seen later that day having a snack lunch at a roadside café on the A40 near Gloucester.

Then for two days nothing. Geoffrey and the Daimler had disappeared.

On Wednesday morning Detective-Superintendent Caswell of Scotland Yard, who was now in charge of the case, called at Garston. A .38 Colt automatic had been found in the garden of Lionel Wallis's cottage and tests had shown that it was the gun from which the two bullets found in the cottage had been fired. Caswell wondered if Mrs Wallis could identify the gun. She did: it was her husband's.

While Caswell was there, a telephone message came through for him. Geoffrey's car had been found abandoned in a field outside the mining town of Aberlandry in South Wales. Caswell told us the news and hurried off.

Julia was excited.

'I know where Geoffrey's hiding. He's got friends in Aberlandry. Will you take me there, Maurice?'

'But Julia, if you think you know where Geoffrey is, you must tell the police.'

She shook her head impatiently.

'I must see him first, Maurice. I promise I'll make him give himself up. But I must see him first.'

I couldn't believe that Geoffrey's friends would harbour him when the whole country knew he was wanted for murder. He wasn't the kind of man to inspire such loyalty.

However, in the end I consented to drive Julia to Aberlandry. To do something positive, however futile, might relieve the strain for her a little.

We had lunch in town and were approaching Aberlandry by 5.30. I pulled up when I spotted the police cars drawn up at the side of the road.

A policeman at once came forward and asked us to drive on. But Julia told him who she was and demanded to see Superintendent Caswell. Just then Caswell himself emerged through a gate from a field on our right.

The flicker of surprise and interest that crossed his face when he saw us was quickly replaced by the customary inscrutability. I recognized in Caswell a formidable character—quiet, efficient, and determined.

He said without preliminaries: 'We've more news for

you, I'm afraid, Mrs Wallis. Your brother-in-law's body has been found.'

Julia caught her breath. After a moment she said: 'Where?'

'Over there,' he replied, pointing. 'In a pond near where your husband's car was found.'

'Is the car still there?'

'Yes.'

Caswell had been talking to us through the open window of my car. Now Julia opened the door and got out.

'I want to see it,' she announced.

Again the swift, appraising look from the superintendent. But he made no comment.

I got out too, and we followed Caswell through the gate and into the field. The Daimler stood some twenty yards away, hidden from the road by the hedge.

Further back from the road the level of the ground dropped and formed a small natural reservoir, perhaps a hundred feet across.

'That's where the body was recovered,' said Caswell, nodding his head towards the water.

'Is it—' Julia began.

'It's in the mortuary in Aberlandry. Now that you're here, we'd like you to identify it, Mrs Wallis, if you feel up to it.'

There was something on Julia's mind. She kept glancing towards the Daimler. Suddenly she turned to the superintendent and said:

'May I see inside the car?'

If Caswell thought the request odd, he gave no sign of it.

'I think so,' he said. 'Just a moment till I have a word with the local chap.'

There were about a dozen policemen in the field, making an inch-by-inch search of the ground. Caswell spoke to the inspector in charge of them. Then he came back to us.

'Yes, that's all right,' he informed Julia. 'The finger-print boys are finished with it, and we've taken all the photographs we need.'

Julia walked over to the Daimler, opened the nearside front door and stood gazing in. Caswell's languid air had dropped from him: he kept close beside Julia and watched her every movement.

When she turned away, she had gone very pale.

'Are you all right, Mrs Wallis?' Caswell enquired solicitously.

'Yes,' she said. 'Yes, I'll be all right. It was seeing that blood on the back seat . . .'

She turned to me: 'Maurice, you knew Lionel. Would you go to the mortuary? It would be too much for me, I'm afraid. If that's all right by the superintendent?'

'Oh! yes. Perfectly all right.' There was the faintest hint of mockery in his voice.

I drove them both in to Aberlandry. Julia got out at the town centre, saying she would call on Geoffrey's friends. She arranged to meet me in an hour. Caswell directed me to the mortuary.

Once before I had had this grisly act to perform, when they fished a student of mine out of the river. It might have been the same mortuary — the long stone corridor on which the footsteps echoed eerily; the phlegmatic, white-coated attendant; the room itself, cold and bare.

Only one of the slabs was occupied. Caswell walked over to it and casually flicked down the sheet.

'Recognize him?' he said.

I recognized him. But it wasn't Lionel Wallis: it was Geoffrey.

CHAPTER 9

'The tragic death of Geoffrey Wallis at the age of 47' (said *The Times* obituary) 'removes untimely from the literary scene one of its most controversial figures. The son of a Scottish miner, he was brought up . . .

'Wallis made his début in literature with the novel *When The Moon Is Low* (1939). Set against the background of the Spanish Civil War, it made an impact only less than Hemingway's *For Whom The Bell Tolls*. Although his later novels, despite their technical mastery, never quite fulfilled the brilliant promise of the first, they were received with increasing popular acclaim. The best-known of them are . . .

'In 1953 Wallis turned to the theatre. His first play, *The Emperor's Clothes*, received universally bad notices; yet it ran to packed houses for nine months. The two plays which followed, in 1954 and 1956, similarly confounded the critics.

'Wallis has been much criticized in recent years for his frequent appearances on television. Serious students of literature have complained that he was sacrificing his talents on the altar of cheap popularity.

'However, perhaps Wallis had the final word. For less than a year ago there was produced at the Vaudeville his last play—the astounding *Kraken Lea*—around which controversy still rages. No less a critic than Henry Fetlock of the *New York Times* has described it as one of the three great plays of this century. Others were less impressed.

'When the dust has settled, what will posterity say of Geoffrey Wallis? *When The Moon Is Low*, one or two of the poems he published at the end of the war, just possibly *Kraken Lea*—these may survive; little else. It is a meagre harvest from one on whom the gods had showered gifts of gold.

'Wallis is survived by his wife (Julia Trant, whom he married in 1939) and two daughters.'

I put down the paper.

'Fairly lukewarm, isn't it?' said Anne.

'It's disgraceful,' Brent exclaimed. 'They should never have got Grossman to write it. What can you expect from a pig but a grunt? He's been green with envy for years.'

I didn't agree with the obituary, but for a different reason. However, I wasn't going to be drawn into a literary argument.

It was the day of the inquest, two days after the finding of Geoffrey's body. At Anne's request I had stayed on at Garston, though I would have liked to slip quietly home. 'There'll be a lot to do,' she said, 'and Philip's not too good in a crisis.'

That proved an understatement. Brent went to pieces when he heard of his employer's death. Julia herself was in bed under sedation.

So it was left to Anne and me to deal with the press, to answer the constantly ringing telephone and doorbell, to negotiate with the police about the inquest and the funeral. Anne was a tower of strength. She packed her sister off to friends, she nursed her mother, and she still had enough composure to discuss the funeral arrangements.

All this time we were waiting for news of Lionel. The police now believed that the driver of the Daimler who had been seen by the garage hand and by the café proprietor on the Sunday had been Lionel. The resemblance between the brothers was close, and people who knew Geoffrey from television and Lionel not at all were very likely to be deceived.

The net was closing round Lionel. Photographs of him had been in every paper, and it was believed he had been seen in Liverpool.

*

The inquest opened with the testimony of the police constable who had found the body. Then I was called to give evidence of identification. The coroner asked me about the last days of Geoffrey's life, particularly the final Saturday. Then I described my visit with Anne to Lionel's cottage on the Sunday evening and what we found there.

The medical evidence was given by the pathologist from Cardiff who had conducted the post-mortem. Death had been caused, he said, by hæmorrhage from bullet wounds in the chest. Four bullets had been fired into Wallis — two had lodged in the chest wall, while the others had passed right through his shoulder. He had died some time between midday Saturday and midday Sunday. The lapse of time before the body was recovered and its immersion in water made it impossible to narrow these limits.

Owen Stryker testified that he had called on Geoffrey at Garston at 3 o'clock on the Saturday and he left half an hour later. On his way back he looked in to see Lionel, as was his habit, and had spent two hours with him, leaving about a quarter to six. Lionel had seemed anxious and depressed and had been drinking steadily all the time Stryker was there. He had mentioned that he was expecting a visit from his brother at 6.15.

Anne was the next witness. She stated that her father had left in his car about 6.10, saying he was going up to town. If in fact, however, he was making for his brother's cottage, he would get there by 6.15, for the distance was only half a mile. Anne herself had left Garston a minute or two before 6.30 and had got to Minford Junction just in time to meet her fiancé's train. She was asked about the Sunday evening and corroborated my account of what we had found at Lionel's cottage.

At this point the Coroner remarked:

'I understand the police have not yet been able to contact Mr Lionel Wallis. Is that so, Superintendent?'

Caswell stood up.

'Well, sir,' he began, 'as a matter of fact—'

But the Coroner interrupted.

'Clearly Mr Wallis will be an important witness at this
inquiry and I therefore propose, with your concurrence,
Superintendent, to adjourn the proceedings for one
week.'

Caswell nodded, and that was that. Julia hadn't been
called at all.

Driving back to Garston we saw a placard outside a
newsagent's shop: 'Wallis found.'

I stopped the car and bought a paper. Lionel had been
picked up in a small hotel in Liverpool.

The front page carried a photograph of him being
escorted from the hotel entrance to a police car. He had
his hand partially over his face, trying to shield it from the
cameras. Between the two strapping policemen he looked
small and defenceless and I had an irrational feeling of
pity for him.

The following day Lionel made a formal appearance in
court to be bound over on a charge of murdering his
brother, Geoffrey Wallis.

PART II

CHAPTER 1

Looking out from the oriel window, I saw the black Morris Minor swing round from the High Street and come to a halt by the pavement below me. Julia Wallis, who had been sitting beside the driver, got out and, after a swift appraising glance at the house, walked up the steps and rang the doorbell. The driver, whose face I couldn't see, remained in his seat.

When Mrs Beddowes showed her in, Julia apologized perfunctorily for being late. She was dressed in black, perhaps as a mark of respect to Geoffrey, but one didn't get the impression of widow's weeds. Her suit had clearly been chosen as an adornment of the living rather than a reminder of the dead.

Mrs Beddowes brought in a trolley with tea. As Julia poured out, I was studying her face. The fortnight that had passed since Geoffrey's funeral had taken some of the furrows from her brow and removed the hunted expression from her eyes. She was relaxed now and more like the Julia of old, arrogant and rather smug.

Tactless, too. Almost her first remark as she gazed round the room was: 'I often wonder why you never married again, Maurice. This can't be much of a life for you.'

I ignored the remark. 'Did you come alone?' I asked her, although I knew she hadn't.

She coloured. 'No, Arthur Durrand's with me. He's teaching me to drive. I got rid of the Daimler and got a small car.'

'Why didn't you bring him in?' I got up and made towards the door.

'No, Maurice, please. He's quite happy to wait in the car. And I want to see you alone.'

Julia had telephoned a couple of nights before to make this appointment. She hadn't said why she wanted to see me. Now she came straight to the point.

'I want you,' she said, 'to do a biography of Geoffrey.'

The suggestion was so bizarre that I had to laugh.

'Good heavens, Julia, that's not in my line at all. Geoffrey moved in a world that's outside my experience. Now, if he'd lived in the eighteenth century—'

'You grew up with him. You understood him. Geoffrey always said you were the only one who understood him.'

'I didn't like him,' I said, more soberly.

'Does a biographer have to *like* his subject? The important thing is to understand him.'

I still couldn't take the proposal seriously.

'Even supposing I were interested, how could I get a publisher? I'll bet Harrington and Leigh have Andrew Clynes sharpening his pencil already.'

'Yes,' Julia conceded, 'Clynes was the man they wanted. But I've persuaded them that you could do it better.'

'You've already discussed this with them?'

'I talked to Owen Stryker last week. He's agreed to publish provided you can promise the manuscript by the end of October.'

'But that's not much more than two months,' I said, appalled. 'Do you know how long I took over *Warren Hastings*? Nearly eight years.'

Julia laughed. 'You didn't have the advantage of personal acquaintance with Mr Hastings. Besides, you'll be writing for a different public this time. They won't expect such scholarly accuracy. The vital thing is to get the book out while the interest is fresh.'

'The interest in what?'

She shrugged impatiently. 'In the trial. Think how it would sell if it appeared about the time of Lionel's conviction.'

At least she was frank. I hadn't believed that even Julia could be so callous.

I still didn't understand why she wanted me to do the biography, nor how she had persuaded a hard-headed publisher to listen to her.

Julia soon cleared up the second point.

'You'll have the diaries to work from, of course. They're mine. Geoffrey left them to me in his will. Nobody can use them without my permission.'

'You mean you forced Stryker's hand by threatening to withhold the diaries?'

She shrugged again. 'I think I was entitled to some say in the matter.'

She glanced at her watch and stood up.

'I really must go, Maurice. Thanks for the tea. I asked Stryker to give you a ring this evening to settle the details.'

She was blandly assuming that I had agreed to write the book.

'I'll think it over, Julia,' I said. Although I had no real intention of accepting, it was against my nature to make a snap decision when I didn't have to.

On her way out Julia paused to look at a photograph of Chris on a table by the window.

'Have you seen Chris recently?' she asked.

'No,' I replied shortly.

'He hasn't been at Garston either since — in the last two weeks. He and Anne seem to have fallen out.'

It was a question rather than a statement. But I didn't want to discuss Chris with Julia.

Chris had pointedly avoided me at the funeral. I noticed, too, a constraint between Anne and him. And he didn't go back to the house from the crematorium.

A night or two later I phoned him from my lodgings, but it was like speaking to a stranger. He was icily polite and unresponsive.

When Chris behaved like that, the diagnosis was usually easy: his mother had been putting ideas about me into his head. But I had thought he had outgrown that phase, for he didn't see so much of Helen now and was less under her influence.

I was disturbed, too, by the signs of a break with Anne. The more I saw of her the more I admired her. Her calmness and clear-headed common sense were exactly the stabilizing influence that Chris needed.

So when Julia casually dropped the remark about Anne and Chris, she unwittingly provided an inducement to me to accept her extraordinary proposal. For if I did accept, it would involve spending much time at Garston. And that might give me the chance to find out what was wrong between Anne and Chris and help put it right.

As I thought it over, the idea of writing the book began to seem less fantastic and more attractive. The unaccustomed idleness of a summer vacation without *Warren Hastings* was already beginning to pall. And if I didn't have the usual qualifications of a popular biographer, at least I had grown up with Geoffrey and, as Julia had said, I understood him, as well as any man was likely to understand so complex a character. I had also read all his work and had strong views on it.

By the time Stryker telephoned, I was half persuaded. He was not friendly. He emphasized that the suggestion had been Julia's, not his, and he barely concealed his disapproval of what he clearly regarded as nepotism.

We arranged to meet at Garston the following day for a full discussion.

CHAPTER 2

'So glad you could come,' Julia said formally, as she led me in. 'Owen Stryker isn't here yet. But Philip'll entertain you.'

'Is Brent still here?' I asked in surprise.

'He hasn't another job to go to, poor boy. I told him he could stay on until something turns up for him. He can help you with the book.'

Julia had taken me into the library. She made a gesture of impatience when she saw the room was empty.

'I *told* him to stay here,' she said petulantly.

Through the window we saw Brent, in sports shirt and slacks, swinging a golf club on the closely mown grass.

Julia pushed open the window.

'Philip!' she called, and her voice was sharp. 'Dr Slater's here. Come and look after him.' Turning to me she added: 'And now, if you'll excuse me—'

'I'm being a nuisance.'

'Not at all. It's just that I hate being so *disorganized*. My help's away for the day and I'm running round in circles.'

'It's a wonder to me you keep this house on at all. Isn't it far too big?'

'That's what Arthur says. He thinks we should sell it.'

I noticed the casual use of Durrand's Christian name and the significant 'we'. And I observed again how much happier Julia looked than when I had last been at Garston.

Philip Brent came into the room then and Julia left us. Brent wasted no time on civilities.

'I hope you realize why they're asking you to do this,' he said, with a sardonic smile. 'They're afraid to employ a professional because they don't want the truth published. They think they can pull the wool over your eyes.'

'The truth about what?' I asked.

He didn't answer me directly.

'You don't see much sign of grief here, do you?' he said. 'She's keeping the remains of the funeral feast in the fridge for the wedding party. But she'll get a shock when I go into the witness-box next week.'

His tone was as offensive as his words. I didn't answer.

When he saw I was displeased, Brent made a grudging apology.

'I'm sorry,' he said, 'but you ought to know how the land lies. Naturally I'll help you all I can. That's my only justification for staying on.'

He pulled open a drawer of the bureau which stood against one wall.

'You'll want to work on the diaries, I expect,' he said. 'They're in the study. But here's an inventory of them that I made out.'

I scanned the list. '1st January-27th March 1927; 28th March-5th June . . .' it began. Each diary covered a period of two to three months. There was, as Stryker had indicated, a gap of two years from the summer of 1936 to the summer of 1938; otherwise the record seemed to be complete right down to the day before Geoffrey's death.

However, a footnote to the inventory stated that a number of entries for specific days were missing from each of the last four diaries (covering the period from November 1961 to July 1962). The dates—about a score of them—were then listed.

'What do you mean by "missing"?' I asked, pointing to Brent's footnote. 'Maybe Geoffrey didn't write anything on these dates.'

'In thirty-five years Mr Wallis never missed a day before.'

'Are you implying that somebody removed these pages?'

'I'm implying nothing,' he said virtuously. 'I've merely recorded that when Mrs Wallis handed over the diaries to me, there were no entries for certain dates. As a matter of fact,' he added, 'there *is* some evidence that at least one of

the pages has been torn out. If you come upstairs, I'll
show you—'

But just then Stryker breezed in. I hadn't heard his car
arrive.

'Well, Professor,' he said, with his customary mock
deference, 'I'd never have guessed you had ambitions to
be a Boswell. We'd better have a talk.'

Brent took the hint and went out.

'I read your book,' Stryker began. 'It's pretty bad.
Wouldn't you agree?'

I nodded. 'I'm not proud of it.'

'Still, you were young at the time. So I've had a peep at
the manuscript of your new one. (Your publishers let me
see it—very irregular, I know.) I don't mind telling you
I'm impressed.'

He had certainly been doing his homework. I realized
now that my commission to write Geoffrey's biography
was far from the *fait accompli* that Julia imagined.

'However,' he went on, 'Geoffrey Wallis is a different
kettle of fish from Warren Hastings. The same technique
would hardly do, would it?'

It was a rhetorical question. I waited.

'Tell me,' he said, 'what do you think of Grossman's
obituary of Geoffrey in *The Times*?'

'Worthless. He missed the essential truth about Geoffrey. They've all missed it.'

Stryker's eyes narrowed, but he didn't interrupt.

'All Geoffrey's work is derivative,' I went on. 'He hadn't
a spark of originality in him. He wasn't found out because
he used so many different sources and so many different
forms. And he was a marvellous copyist. He could have
written a play in the manner of Shakespeare which the
Bard himself wouldn't have been ashamed of. In fact he
did, while he was at University.

'Whether such a man could ever be a great writer I
don't know. It's been said that some of van Meegeren's

paintings are just as great as those of the master whose style he was slavishly imitating. But Geoffrey—'

I broke off in confusion, because Stryker was grinning at me. I had been speaking as if I were addressing a class of students.

'OK, Professor, you've made your point.' His voice was warmer than before. 'You're the first man who's talked sense to me about Wallis as a writer. Now I think we might get down to business. We can offer . . .'

'I'm told,' said Julia, at lunch, 'that Lionel's going to plead not guilty.'

'Where did you hear that?' asked Stryker.

'Well, Arthur—'

'Ah! yes, Arthur. Trust him to nose it out.'

There was an awkward silence. Then Julia tried again.

'You'll be giving evidence Owen?'

'I believe so. Why?'

'I just wondered . . . You left the cottage about six o'clock, didn't you?'

He put down his fork and stared at her.

'5.45. I said so at the inquest.'

'You didn't see—no, of course not, you couldn't have.'

'See what?'

'Well, I wondered if perhaps you'd seen Geoffrey arrive. But, of course, if you left as early as that . . .' Her voice tailed off.

Stryker continued to stare at her.

'You were never out that day, Julia, were you?' he asked.

For some reason she was flustered by the question.

'I—no, I—it was so hot. I didn't feel well. I had to lie down.'

It was a curious exchange, in which what was left unspoken seemed to have more meaning than the words themselves. On the face of it Julia was the more upset. But Stryker too had been put off his stride and was uncharacteristically silent for the rest of the meal.

CHAPTER 3

On Julia's invitation I moved to Garston for the rest of the summer. Geoffrey's study was set aside for my use.

Of Julia herself I saw little. We were both busy during the day and in the evenings she was nearly always out. Anne was only at Garston at the week-ends, and Jane was still away staying with friends.

I was perforce thrown much into the company of Philip Brent. I soon modified my first impression of him. Vain, pretentious and over-sensitive, he was, nevertheless, something of an idealist and he was fiercely loyal to anyone who had been kind to him. Above all to Geoffrey.

Once he was satisfied that my aim was to tell the truth about Geoffrey and not just to build up a sensational story, Philip couldn't have been more co-operative. He assembled in chronological order all Geoffrey's publications, including even ephemeral stuff like newspaper articles and television scripts. Then he tracked down, mostly in libraries in Cambridge and London, everything — or nearly everything — that had been written *about* Geoffrey, especially reviews of his books and plays. Although Geoffrey had kept a file of press cuttings, he must have been selective, because there were no unfavourable ones. Brent was admirably thorough in filling the gaps.

Meanwhile I was wading stolidly through the diaries. They began in 1927 when Geoffrey was twelve, and for the first three years or so they were the conventional chronicle of events in a schoolboy's life. I recognized these little red notebooks with the immature handwriting, for I had been there when Geoffrey wrote them and I had occasionally dipped into them in his absence. I re-read them now with nostalgia.

About 1930 a change began to creep in. It was about that time, I recalled now, that Geoffrey had taken to hiding his diary from me. I could readily understand why. The happenings of the day were treated as pegs on which to hang a dissection of the characters concerned. There were precociously perceptive and cruel portraits of the people I had known in Bresford in my youth, my parents, my school friends, pinned and labelled like butterflies. I came off better than most, I suppose. 'Dull and plodding' was how he summed me up.

The savage portraits continued down the years, and none of his friends or acquaintances escaped the lash. There was even a cold and unsympathetic appraisal of Julia, his wife.

As Geoffrey's stock in the world of literature had risen, the names of the famous obtruded more and more. If Geoffrey said to their faces one tenth of what he wrote in the diaries about them, his unpopularity with his fellow artists was understandable. He brought under the microscope not only their personal idiosyncrasies but also their published work; and I soon recognized that as a literary critic he had had outstanding perceptiveness and taste.

For the biographer the chief interest in the diaries lay in their frank revelation of the sources of Geoffrey's inspiration. Every incident that happened to him, every book he read, every interesting conversation he listened to — they were all carefully docketed for possible future use.

It was hard to understand why Geoffrey should ever have wanted these diaries published in his lifetime. Even after the excision of libellous matter, they could have done nothing but harm to his reputation, for they revealed the poverty of his imaginative gifts and the extent of his unacknowledged debt to other writers for form and language and, in some cases, even incident and characters.

Until almost the end the diaries were characterized by a devastating candour. You felt that what you were reading was the truth as Geoffrey saw it and that nothing was being held back. In the last few months, however, odd cryptic sentences began to appear, hinting at some impending event which he was awaiting with anxious fascination. There was no clue to what it was. One got the impression not that he was being secretive but that his readers were expected to know all about it already.

It was in this final period, too, that—as Brent's inventory showed—several dates were missing altogether. The diaries were loose-leaf notebooks, of varying sizes and colours—cheap notebooks that could be bought at any stationer's. Geoffrey had written on one side of the paper only and had started each day on a fresh page. Many of the entries were of only a line or two; others covered several pages. But until the end of 1961 there was never a day without an entry of some sort (apart from the two years from June 1936 for which there were no diaries at all).

The first of the missing dates was 24th December 1961; then, 16th, 17th and 18th February 1962, then 9th March, and after that, at irregular intervals, three or four days each month.

I spoke to Brent about it again.

'You said you had some evidence that these pages had been torn out. What was it?'

He took the second last of the diaries and opened it at 25th May. There was no entry for the 24th, but Brent pointed to a tiny scrap of paper adhering to the spiral of wire which bound the pages.

'There was a page here that's been removed,' he pointed out.

A thought struck me.

'Wasn't it about then that Lionel had a quarrel with Julia and had to leave Garston?'

'No, that happened earlier. First Saturday in May, I remember. That's funny, though'—Brent had been flicking back the pages of the diary—'that date *is* missing too.

Saturday, 5th May. What made you think of that?'

'It just seemed odd,' I said, 'that Geoffrey never mentioned in his diary his brother's arrival or departure. Then I remembered it was last Christmas Eve that Lionel came to Garston, and that's the first of the missing dates. That made me wonder when exactly he left here. But what about the other dates that are missing—can you remember anything special happening on any of them?'

He looked at the list—his own list—and frowned in concentration.

'16th, 17th, 18th February. It was just about then that Mr Wallis suddenly gave up writing. In fact,'—he was consulting his own pocket diary—'16th is exactly the date.'

Brent had been in London that day completing the arrangements for a lecture tour in the States that Geoffrey was to make. When he got back to Garston in the evening he found that Geoffrey had gone to bed and the others were sitting around 'like mourners at a wake'.

'Who was there?' I interrupted.

'Just Mrs Wallis and Lionel and Mr Durrand.'

They wouldn't tell Brent what had happened, but it was clear that there had been a tremendous row.

'Even Lionel was subdued,' said Brent. 'It was the strangest thing to see them sitting there. Like mourners at a wake,' he repeated.

Next day Geoffrey had cancelled his American tour. He seemed to have changed overnight: all his zest had gone. He had lost the urge to write.

'Have you still no idea what had happened?' I asked.

Brent hesitated.

'Well,' he said finally, 'it had something to do with Mrs Wallis. They scarcely spoke to each other after that. And another thing: Mr Durrand was never back at Garston after that night, except when Mr Wallis was away.'

The first Sunday morning after my return to Garston I was

out walking and, without conscious intent, found myself turning down the side road that led to Lionel's cottage.

Seeing a bicycle propped against the wall of the cottage, I was sufficiently curious to go up and look through a window.

Arthur Durrand came out.

'Oh! it's you, Maurice,' he said ungraciously; then, after a perceptible pause: 'You'd better come in.'

Order had been restored to the sitting-room, and it was here that Durrand took me.

'The police are finished here now,' he said. 'I was just taking a quick look round to see what the damage is.'

He offered a cigarette but didn't ask me to sit down.

'Has Lionel given up the tenancy?' I asked innocently.

'Well—not exactly. He'd paid to the end of September. But I've got the owner's interests to safeguard. I'm perfectly entitled to come here any time.'

'And go through the tenant's private papers?' I said, nodding at the heap of papers on the table.

He gave a half-hearted laugh.

'You're too observant, old boy. Sit down and I'll tell you about it.'

He didn't sit down himself, but paced up and down as he spoke, his hands behind his back. It was a practised pose; no doubt the one he used when dictating at his office.

'I have it on good authority,' he began—the pompous cliché tripped naturally from his tongue—'that Lionel's defence will be an attempt to prove that someone else did it.'

'Not a very original defence.'

'You don't take my point. He's going to try to prove that someone *specific* did it.'

'Who?'

He ignored my question.

'My grapevine also tells me that part of the evidence on which the defence will rely is the whisky that Lionel and Geoffrey drank that night.'

'Your grapevine knows too much. Where *did* you pick all this up, Arthur?'

He shrugged and said: 'Pearce and Pearce are Lionel's solicitors and one of their clerks let it out to my chief clerk. They want him to plead provocation or self-defence, but he won't hear of it. He insists he's not guilty and of course they've got to take his instructions. He hasn't a hope in Hades of succeeding.' But Durrand sounded worried all the same.

'What's the significance of the whisky?' I asked.

'God knows. It eludes me.'

'And these papers you've been rifling through?'

He stopped his restless perambulation and gazed owlishly at me.

'Have you ever worked out what happened that night? Geoffrey came down here with a gun, there was a struggle, Lionel got hold of the gun and shot him and then made off with the body. All right. But what was Geoffrey after? My belief is he came to recover whatever Lionel was blackmailing him with. Some kind of incriminating document, no doubt. Only Lionel moved too fast for him.'

'And you're looking for the document? Surely if there was anything like that, the police would have found it.'

'They might not see its significance. I just want to be *sure* there's nothing here . . .'

'And is there?' I asked.

'No,' he said shortly.

I returned to his earlier evasion.

'Who is it that Lionel's accusing? Is it you, Arthur?'

He was visibly shaken.

'Me? Good heavens, no . . . How could anyone imagine — Besides, I was never out that day. I pottered around the garden all afternoon . . . No, it's Julia that he's trying to pin it on.'

I had guessed as much.

He went over to the table, gathered up the papers and

bundled them into an empty drawer that was lying on the floor.

'That's how he kept his correspondence,' he said with distaste. 'All stuffed together in the one drawer—letters and accounts and receipts and circulars.'

He carried the drawer through to another room and I could hear it being rammed back into the desk or chest from which it had been pulled out.

We left together a few minutes later.

We walked up towards the main road, Durrand pushing his bicycle and panting a little from the exertion. Eventually he had to stop to get his breath.

'A nice spot for camping,' I remarked, pointing back down the valley.

'Yes, it would be, but Sir John doesn't allow it.'

'I don't know who Sir John is, but I've seen campers there.'

'Oh! no. Sir John Cressey owns all this land south-east of Gleeve. He won't tolerate campers. And his estate agent can nose them out from a mile away.'

'Damn it, Arthur, the last time I was here there was a tent pitched down by the river, not fifty yards from the cottage.'

Durrand looked worried.

'You mean at the time Geoffrey was murdered?'

'Well, it was certainly there when Stryker and I visited Lionel a day or two before that. Two young girls, I think.'

He made no further comment and we resumed our climb.

When we reached the main road, Durrand prepared to get on his bicycle. Then he changed his mind and turned to me again.

'Have you seen your son lately?' he asked.

'No.'

'I understand,' he said slowly, feeling for his words, 'that he's to be a witness for the defence, so to speak.'

'What do you mean?'

'Pearce and Pearce seem to think he has some evidence which might help their client. I wish you'd speak to him and tell him not to be a fool, Maurice. It won't do him any good, you know.'

And now he had mounted, somewhat precariously, and, with a wave of the hand that almost unseated him, made off along the road to the village.

CHAPTER 4

Earlier that week, getting no reply from Chris's lodgings, I had phoned the hotel in which he was working and learned that he was on a week's holiday. They weren't able to give me an address.

Anne came home as usual for the weekend. When I spoke to her about Chris, her replies were monosyllabic and I learned nothing except that things were not going smoothly between them. She drifted about unhappily all day Saturday and most of Sunday, as if hoping Chris might appear. Eventually, late on the Sunday afternoon, she packed her bag and drove back to London.

If she had waited an hour longer, she would have seen Chris. I was sitting in the garden, toying with *Ximenes*, when, about six o'clock, a figure in khaki shirt and shorts, with haversack on back, toiled up the drive. He was deeply tanned and his fair hair was bleached by the sun.

When he saw me, he hesitated momentarily before coming over.

'Is Anne here?' he asked.

'You've just missed her.'

'Damn!'

'He brought over a chair and sat down beside me. His manner was wary.

'Where have you been?' I asked him.

'Hitchhiking in Wales. I did some climbing—and I visited Aberlandry.'

'Aberlandry? Why?'

'Just a hunch . . . Dad, when you took Mrs Wallis to Aberlandry that day, where did she go while you were at the mortuary?'

'Well, she said Geoffrey had friends in Aberlandry who might know where he was.'

'I know who those friends are. They're actually cousins of *Mrs* Wallis. I met them when they visited Garston at Easter. Two elderly spinsters. The last people to harbour a wanted murderer. Mrs Wallis couldn't really have believed her husband would be there.'

'But—'

'I called on them. Mrs Wallis did go there when she left you. She was in quite a state, they said. She blurted out that her husband was dead and then later, when she was calmer, she said they'd misunderstood her—it was her brother-in-law who was dead and her husband was wanted for his murder.'

'You mean that Julia had already guessed it was Geoffrey and not Lionel who'd been murdered even before I identified the body?'

' "Guessed" isn't the word I would have chosen.'

'Be careful what you're saying, Chris.'

'Oh! I might have known you'd defend her,' he retorted angrily.

The bitterness in his voice should have warned me. But I was angry myself.

'Look here, Chris,' I said, 'you're practically accusing Julia of being accessory to a murder. What's Anne going to think of that?'

'Anne and I are through anyway. I came here today to tell her. I've thought of nothing else for the past week and I know now it wouldn't work.'

'But why, Chris?'

He stared at me.

'*You* ask me that, Dad?'

I was taken aback by the ferocity of his tone.

The front door of the house opened and Julia's voice called: 'Maurice!'

Chris got up abruptly.

'I must go. I don't want to meet her.'

'Where are you making for?'

'Minford. I must get back tonight. I start work tomorrow.'

'Well, let me drive you to the station.'

'No, thanks, Dad. I'll walk.' His voice brooked no argument.

I watched him as he crossed the lawn and plodded down the drive.

Julia was still at the door. Now she came over and joined me.

'That was Chris, wasn't it?' she asked as she sank into the deck chair he had left. 'Why didn't he stay?'

'He only came to see Anne,' I said shortly.

Julia took a deep breath. 'I hope you won't be offended, Maurice,' she began (like many tactless people, she believed that a preamble like that gave her licence to say anything) 'but I've now quite made up my mind that Chris isn't a suitable person for Anne to marry. And I won't permit it.'

'What's wrong with him?' I asked, keeping my temper in check.

Even Julia had qualms about putting her objections into words. But she did.

'Well, one wouldn't mind him being poor, if he had some prospects. But, frankly, Maurice, I won't have Anne throwing herself away on someone whose ultimate goal is to be manager of a hotel.'

I didn't answer. There was no arguing with Julia on such a subject.

All the same I was angry and I chose a more vulnerable point to attack her.

'Julia,' I said, 'when did you first know that Geoffrey was dead?'

'You told me—that day in Aberlandry—after you'd been to the mortuary.'

'You knew before then, though, didn't you?'

Julia looked at me speculatively. I think she was wondering whether she could brazen it out.

'Give me a cigarette, Maurice,' she said.

When it was lit, she went on:

'I knew Geoffrey was going to see Lionel that weekend. When I discovered his revolver was missing from his desk I even wondered whether he might be planning to murder him. He was ruthless enough for it. But if Geoffrey had ever committed a crime, it would have been planned to the last detail. He'd never have left a trail of clues across the country, he wouldn't have bought petrol at three in the morning or parked his car beside the lorries at a roadside café.

'That's why I suspected almost from the start that it was Geoffrey who was dead and Lionel who was on the run. And I knew it for certain when the superintendent let me look inside the car at Aberlandry. Whoever had been driving that car, it wasn't Geoffrey.'

'How did you know?'

'Well, years ago Geoffrey went into a shop and left his car on the slope outside. He'd forgotten to put on the hand-brake, and when he came out, the car was piled against a lamppost at the foot of the hill. Ever since then, when he parked the car, even on the level, he always left it in gear as an extra precaution. He had a phobia about it. But when I looked inside the Daimler at Aberlandry, the gear lever was in neutral. That's why I didn't want to go to the mortuary.'

It was plausible. Yet there was something strained about her manner, as if she feared a further, and more awkward, question.

'How's the book going, Maurice?' she asked, changing the subject.

I hadn't yet written a line of the biography. I had spent the first week reading the diaries and taking notes. During the week that followed I read (or, rather, re-read) everything Geoffrey had ever published, from his first novel down to *Kraken Lea*; then I ploughed through Philip Brent's file of press cuttings—book reviews, dramatic criticisms, profiles, gossip paragraphs. I learned many new facts, but nothing that radically altered my own picture of Geoffrey as an artist and a person.

My next task was to talk to Geoffrey's friends and associates, especially people in the theatre and television with whom he had worked in recent years. I put Brent on to arranging appointments.

There was still one puzzling gap to be filled—the two years or so after Geoffrey came down from University. Not only was there no diary for these years, his published writings gave no clue, except possibly *When The Moon Is Low*, which some critics believed to be partly autobiographical.

Owen Stryker was beginning to show anxiety.

'It's nearly the end of August already,' he pointed out on one occasion, 'and we want—'

'I know. You want the manuscript by the end of October. You'll get it. But I must do the groundwork first.'

He shook his head doubtfully. However, he made a useful suggestion when I spoke of the two years' hiatus in my material on Geoffrey.

'Did you notice when the diary breaks off in 1936?' he said.

'Yes. On the day he went down from University.'

'Quite. But he didn't go abroad till the beginning of August. What was he doing in the month in between?'

I had wondered about that myself. Casting my mind back twenty-five years, I had the hazy impression that Geoffrey had just returned from holiday somewhere when he made his announcement that he was leaving the country.

'Yes, he was on holiday,' Stryker agreed. 'He was staying with his brother and his uncle in Scotland. Lionel told me that himself, though he wouldn't say what happened. But *something* happened there, something that forced Geoffrey to beat it hotfoot across the channel. If I were you, I'd go up to Scotland and ferret around.'

CHAPTER 5

The first two days of the trial at court followed the expected pattern: the prosecution built up an impressive case against Lionel, the defence held its fire, and the reporters were hard-pressed to infuse drama into so one-sided an engagement.

The prosecution's case was formidable. Evidence was given that the bullets which killed Geoffrey had been fired from a revolver found in the garden of the cottage and that the only fingerprints on the revolver were Lionel's; his prints had also been found on the steering-wheel of the Daimler; and a suit of bloodstained clothes, identified as having belonged to him, had been found hidden in a copse near where the car was abandoned. In addition, nearly a dozen witnesses swore to having seen Lionel at various stages of the flight from Gleeve to Aberlandry.

All this time I had been watching Lionel Wallis in the dock. The likeness to Geoffrey was even more apparent when, as now, you could see only head and shoulders and the difference in height was obscured. He was taking a lively interest in the proceedings and from time to time would scribble a note on a pad and pass it across to his counsel.

Percy Hocking had been engaged for the defence. When he took silk fifteen years before, Hocking was being confidently tipped for future elevation to the bench, but indifferent health had been his stumbling-block. A thin, swarthy man, with a quiet voice and no mannerisms, he seemed insignificant and ineffectual beside the swash-buckling Sir Edward Kissack, who was leader for the prosecution.

Hocking sat impassive, arms folded and eyes half-closed, through the long succession of Crown witnesses. The only one he cross-examined in these first two days was Superintendent Caswell, and then on what seemed a minor point.

'Superintendent,' he said, 'when you described what you found in the sitting-room of the cottage, you mentioned two empty glasses on the mantelshelf. Did you mean literally empty?'

'I don't underst—oh! I see. No, sir, there were dregs of whisky in them.'

'You had the liquid analysed?'

'Yes, sir.'

'And it was pure whisky?'

'No, diluted with soda.'

'In both glasses?'

'Yes, sir.'

'You had the glasses tested for fingerprints, I take it?'

'Yes. One had the prints of the deceased, and the other of the accused.'

'Of which hand?'

'The right hand in each case. Both men were right-handed, I understand.'

'Thank you, Superintendent, but please confine yourself to answering my questions. Were there no other
prints on either of the glasses?'

Caswell paused before he answered. He seemed suddenly to have scented a trap.

'Well, sir,' he said cautiously, 'you'll appreciate that I
didn't test the glasses myself. Detective-Sergeant Phillips
will be giving evidence later and perhaps . . .'

'Very well,' said Hocking, dismissing him.

In due course Sergeant Phillips testified that no other
identifiable prints had been found on either of the
glasses.

The official theory of how the murder had been committed gradually emerged. It was suggested that Lionel had
some hold over his brother and was blackmailing him,
that Geoffrey went to the cottage on the night of the
murder to try to persuade or to compel Lionel to desist
from the blackmail, that he produced a revolver and
threatened his brother with it, that there was a struggle in
the course of which Lionel obtained possession of the gun,
and that Lionel shot Geoffrey. He then tried to delay
discovery of the murder by taking the body away in Geoffrey's car and dumping it in an isolated spot in Wales.

There was abundant evidence to support most of this.
Geoffrey had made no secret of his dislike of his brother
and had hinted to several people that Lionel was blackmailing him. Owen Stryker testified that Lionel was expecting his brother that evening and in my own evidence I
recounted the conversation I had overheard between the
two brothers fixing an appointment for 6.15. There seemed
no reasonable doubt that when Geoffrey left Garston at
6.10, it was to his brother's cottage he was going.

Julia was the last witness for the prosecution. There was
the usual stir and murmur of interest when the victim's
widow goes into the box. Lionel laid down his pencil and

fixed his gaze unwaveringly on her. Even Hocking, I thought, looked more alert than he had all day.

Kissack took her sympathetically through the last months of her husband's life. She described how Lionel had descended on Garston last Christmas and the five months he had spent with them.

'Was he a welcome guest, Mrs Wallis?'

'On the contrary. We all disliked him.'

'Then why—?'

'My husband was afraid of him.'

'Do you know why?'

'Lionel had some hold over him. It concerned something that happened a long time ago, Geoffrey told me.'

Julia was asked about the incident that led to Lionel's dismissal from Garston in May. Her reply was slower, a little less confident, and I noticed that she carefully turned her eyes away from her brother-in-law in the dock.

'He made an improper suggestion to me,' she said.

Kissack didn't ask her to elaborate.

'Do you recognize this gun, Mrs Wallis?' He handed her the .38 Colt automatic previously identified as the murder weapon.

Julia turned it over briefly.

'Yes,' she said, 'it's Geoffrey's.'

'When did you last see it?'

'Superintendent Caswell showed it—'

'No, I mean, before that?'

'A week, ten days perhaps, before Geoffrey's death. I don't remember exactly. He kept it in his desk in the study.'

'When did you first notice it was missing?'

'On the Saturday night—the night Geoffrey disappeared. I was worried when he didn't come home that night. I guessed he'd gone to see Lionel and I was afraid he might have done something foolish. That's why I looked to see if his gun was still there.'

'You mean you thought he might have taken the gun in order to shoot his brother?'

'No, not that. But I was afraid he might have used it to *threaten* Lionel, and—well, accidents do happen.'

All the drama was reserved for the second day. Julia had finished her evidence-in-chief the previous afternoon and seemed surprised to be recalled for cross-examination.

Hocking's first question electrified the court.

'Mrs Wallis, did you murder your husband?'

Kissack was on his feet at once, protesting, but Julia cut him short.

'I don't mind answering,' she said, looking contemptuously at Hocking. 'The answer is "no".'

'You did, however, on at least one occasion threaten to murder him?'

'I don't know what you're talking about.'

The answer had come promptly and confidently. But I knew Julia. I had seen the flicker of alarm that flashed across her face.

'Well, let me refresh your memory. Do you remember the evening of 8th July?'

'That's two months ago. How could I—'

'It was rather a special day, though. A Sunday—the day your daughter became engaged. Doesn't that bring it back?'

'Yes,' she admitted grudgingly.

'You had a quarrel with your husband that night, didn't you?'

There was a significant pause before she answered.

'I believe we did have words.'

'You shouted at each other?'

'I'm perfectly sure we did not. It was just a minor difference of opinion.'

'What were you discussing?'

'I don't remember . . . Oh! yes, I do—it was about my

daughter and her—her fiancé. Geoffrey and I didn't see
eye-to-eye on the engagement.'

That was a transparent invention. Julia was no actress
and when she told a falsehood, her face and her voice
betrayed her. But Hocking let it pass.

'In the course of this minor difference of opinion, Mrs
Wallis, did you call your husband "insane" and "a
monster"?'

'One uses extravagant terms when one is angry.'

'Did you also say that you would put a bullet in him
rather than let him persist in a certain course of conduct?'

'I don't remember,' Julia muttered.

Hocking stared at her.

'You don't remember? Tell me, Mrs Wallis, how did
you and your husband get on as a general rule? Latterly, I
mean—say, in the last six months?'

Kissack intervened again.

'I really must protest, your Honour. These questions
have no relevance to—'

The scrawny little man on the bench stopped him.

'I think, Sir Edward, that the defence must have
reasonable latitude in developing its case.' He nodded to
Hocking. 'Proceed, Mr Hocking.'

Hocking smiled deprecatingly.

'Thank you, your Honour. However, since my learned
friend takes exception, I'll not press the question.'

He turned back to Julia.

'How well do you know Mr Arthur Durrand?'

The switch in the attack brought no relief to Julia.

'He's—he was my husband's lawyer. We've been friends
for many years.'

'You still see a good deal of him?'

'I—yes. He lives close by and, as I say, he's a friend of
the family.'

'A friend of the family,' Hocking repeated, as though
the words held some sinister meaning. Kissack was

fidgeting, ready to pounce.

But Hocking suddenly switched direction again.

'Mrs Wallis,' he said, 'you told us that my client, the accused'—he pointed to Lionel in the dock, and Julia's eyes
involuntarily followed his arm—'you told us that he made
an improper suggestion to you and that that's why he was
dismissed from your house. Would you be more explicit
about the incident?'

Julia didn't answer. She was staring at Lionel as if she
couldn't tear her eyes away.

Hocking's tone hardened.

'I put it to you that the reason your brother-in-law left
Garston was quite different, that he found out about the
affair between you and—'

He wasn't allowed to finish the sentence. This time
Kissack's objection was sustained and the question was
struck from the record.

Hocking patiently waited till the hubbub had died
down. He had achieved his object. No one in that court
had any doubt that it was being suggested that Arthur
Durrand and Julia were lovers, and had been even while
Geoffrey was alive.

The cross-examination ended on a quieter note.

'Where were you between 4.30 and 7 o'clock on the
afternoon of 28th July?'

'In my room.'

'The whole time?'

'The whole time.'

Hocking briefly addressed the court. His client was innocent, he said, and reserved his defence. For certain
reasons, however, it was important that the evidence of
one witness for the defence should be put on record now.
He therefore called Christopher Robert Slater.

Chris was an earnest witness, with so scrupulous a
regard for the exact truth that sometimes the pause

before he answered was painfully prolonged.

He spoke of his journey to Garston on the Saturday evening Geoffrey had disappeared. His train had got into Minford a minute or two late. Anne was waiting in her car and drove him to Garston, as she always did.

'Did you see anyone you recognized in the course of that drive?' Hocking asked him.

'Yes, I saw—'

'First of all, where was this?'

'At the crossroads just before Gleeve.' Chris described the junction—the road to the right leading down to Lionel Wallis's cottage, and to the left to Upper Cresswell Farm and to the back entrance to Garston.

'When you were passing that junction you saw someone you knew?'

'I saw Mrs Wallis.'

There was a ripple of excited comment, quickly silenced by the Clerk of the Court.

'What was she doing?'

'She was on her bicycle on the farm road to my left, cycling back towards Garston.'

'Let me get this clear,' said Hocking. 'You were sitting beside the driver and as you passed the intersection you looked up the road to your left and saw Mrs Wallis on her bicycle?'

'Yes.'

'How far away was she when you saw her?'

'Twenty yards, perhaps thirty yards.'

'But you were in no doubt who it was?'

'None at all.'

'What time was this, Mr Slater?'

'About 6.55. We left Minford just after a quarter to seven, and we'd gone about five miles.'

'And Mrs Wallis was cycling away from you, towards the rear entrance to Garston?'

'Yes.'

'Where had she come from?'

Chris shrugged. 'I don't know,' he said.

'Well, let me put it like this. Suppose someone was leaving Mr Lionel Wallis's cottage and wanted to cycle back to Garston, wouldn't the quickest way be to cross the main road and go up the Cresswell Farm road just as you saw Mrs Wallis doing —'

Sir Edward Kissack's blood pressure was up again and his indignant objection was sustained. But once again Hocking had got his point across.

He turned to something quite different.

'You know the defendant, Mr Lionel Wallis?'

Chris looked towards the dock.

'Not well,' he said. 'I met him a number of times at Garston.'

'Have you observed his drinking habits?'

'I'm afraid I don't understand.'

'Well, would you describe him as a heavy drinker, a moderate drinker, or perhaps a teetotaller?'

Chris permitted himself a rare smile.

'Not a teetotaller anyway. Until today I've never seen him without a glass of whisky by his side.'

'Whisky and soda?'

'No, he took it neat, any time I saw him.'

Unexpectedly Hocking sat down.

In his cross-examination, counsel for the Crown made one of his rare psychological errors in summing up a witness. He could have neutralized Chris's evidence by getting him to admit that, having seen the cyclist only for a second as the car flashed past the intersection, he might have been mistaken in thinking he recognized Julia. Instead, Kissack chose to regard Chris as a dishonest witness seeking to discredit Julia out of personal spite.

From the first question his manner was hostile.

'This cyclist that you say you saw — did your fiancée see her also?'

'No. At least, she didn't mention it.'

'A pity . . . By the way, Miss Wallis still is your fiancée, I take it?'

'No. We've broken off the engagement.'

The famous eyebrows were up in exaggerated surprise.

'Really? May one ask why?'

Chris flushed but didn't answer.

'Well, far be it from me to probe. But tell me this: was Mrs Wallis enamoured of you as a future son-in-law?'

'She didn't approve of the engagement, if that's what you mean.'

'That's precisely what I mean. And, more than that, it was she who persuaded her daughter to break it off, wasn't it?'

'No. That was entirely between Anne and me. We—'

But Kissack was going on as if Chris hadn't spoken.

'So that your feelings towards Mrs Wallis are not of the friendliest?'

Again Chris didn't answer.

'Mrs Wallis has sworn that she was in her room that afternoon from 4.30 till after 7. Are you telling the Court that she's a liar?'

Chris said: 'I simply described what I saw. If it doesn't agree with somebody else's evidence, that's no business of mine.'

Under pressure from Kissack, Chris's earlier hesitancy had gone and he was now answering crisply and confidently. Kissack saw the red light and began to back-pedal; his next few questions were harmless fill-ins.

A paper was handed to counsel by his junior. Kissack read it with a puzzled frown and glanced over at the public gallery. Then, hitching his gown over his shoulders, he turned back to Chris.

'Mr Slater, you told us you reached Minford Junction at 6.40 or thereabouts. What time did your train leave London?'

'5.59.'

'That's an express, isn't it?'

'Yes. Minford's the first stop.'

'It didn't stop anywhere before Minford that night?'

'No.'

Kissack glanced again at the public gallery, as if looking for inspiration. Then he added a casual question.

'What were you doing earlier that afternoon?'

Chris had paused so regularly before answering a question that the delay this time was only fractionally longer than usual. But I knew the difference at once and, when he did speak, I recognized that for the first time he was lying.

'I was working,' he said. 'I was on duty till 5 o'clock.'

CHAPTER 6

I met Arthur Durrand outside the Court. He was waiting for Julia.

'By God!' he said. 'That's a bloody scandal. The man ought to be struck off.' He was seething.

'Who? Hocking?'

'Yes, Hocking. In all the years I've been attending courts I've never heard a performance like that. Of course, he should never have got away with it! I can't imagine what old Jessop was thinking of, letting him go on.'

I had some sympathy with Durrand. From the flimsiest evidence Hocking had woven a web of suspicion round Julia.

'Why did he bother?' I asked. 'It didn't do any good. Why didn't he keep his secret weapon for the trial itself?'

Durrand scowled. 'He's got what he wanted. Julia's name's been dragged in the mud. People are beginning to

wonder if Lionel's been victimized. And if the jury starts
off feeling sorry for him, that's half Hocking's battle
won.'

Durrand appeared to be more worried than the circumstances warranted. After all, the defence had scarcely
made a dent in the case against Lionel.

'You do believe Lionel's guilty?' I asked.

He gave an oblique answer. 'I wish I knew what Hocking's got up his sleeve. I'm told the police aren't too
happy.'

Just then Julia emerged from the court house and came
down the steps to join us.

'Well, Maurice,' she said, 'I hope you're proud of your
son.'

'You can't blame Chris for telling what he saw.'

Julia sniffed. 'It's a funny thing he's only telling it now.
He never said a word at the time. He'll regret this,
though, won't he, Arthur?'

Durrand was suddenly anxious to be off.

'Julia and I are having dinner in town,' he remarked,
glancing at his watch. 'So, if you'll excuse us . . .'

He shepherded her to his car and they drove off. It was
only 4.15. A little early for him to be in a hurry for a
dinner engagement.

Just then I noticed a Consul parked behind where Durrand's had been. Anne was in the driver's seat. When I
went over she put down the window.

'I'm waiting for Chris,' she said.

'Chris? But he's away. He slipped out as soon as he'd
finished his evidence.'

'Damn! I was counting on seeing him.'

There was a catch in her voice and I saw her eyes fill
with tears.

'Are you coming down to Garston this weekend, Anne?'
I asked.

'No, I—I think I'll stay in town.'

'Well, let's go for tea somewhere. I'd like to talk to you about Chris.'

She looked at me uncertainly and then gave a pleased nod.

'That would be lovely. But why not come back to my flat? It'll be easier to talk there.'

My car was parked across the road. I got into it and followed her as she threaded her way through the traffic.

She lived in a first-floor flat in a quiet cul-de-sac off Earl's Court Road. It wasn't the sort of place I had expected. The furnishings of the room that she took me into were heavy, old-fashioned and drab. The only imprints of Anne's personality that I could see were the gay Picasso reproductions on the wall, some coloured cushions and a framed photograph of Chris on what seemed to be an old gramophone cabinet.

'Disappointed?' said Anne, her eyes twinkling. 'Chris calls it the morgue. It's cheap, though. That's the only reason I stay.'

She read another unspoken question in my face, for she continued: 'I'm not well off, you know. I never let Dad give me an allowance. I'd rather be independent. The car's the one extravagance—that was a gift from Dad when I got my first job.'

While Anne was away making tea, I examined the books in the big mahogany bookcase. One shelf consisted entirely of Geoffrey's works. Picking one out at random, (it was the published text of *Kraken Lea*), I saw that the title page had been inscribed by Geoffrey 'To my darling Anne, the only one I can trust—March, 1962.' This odd inscription so intrigued me that I pulled out several of the other volumes; but on all of them Geoffrey had written, more conventionally, 'To Anne, with love' or words to that effect.

I still had *Kraken Lea* in my hand when Anne came in with the tea. She had changed from the black suit she had been wearing into a summer dress.

She glanced swiftly at the book and coloured slightly when she saw the page at which it was open.

'Dad was feeling sorry for himself when he wrote that,' she remarked. 'Sugar, Dr Slater?'

She poured out.

'Yes,' she went on, 'he wasn't himself these last months. He had too much on his mind.'

'Lionel?'

She hesitated. 'Perhaps . . . No, it's silly to say that. He wasn't really too bothered about Uncle Lionel. I'm sure he was just waiting for the right moment to deal with him. Do you remember we talked about this the day you arrived at Garston? I told you about Dad being black-mailed by Uncle Lionel and I think I said that wasn't his only worry. I couldn't very well say more then, when I hardly knew you, but the truth is, what really broke him up was finding out about Mother and that—that man Durrand.'

'It was true, then, what was hinted in court today about Durrand and your mother?'

Anne sighed. 'Everybody knew it, even Jane. They weren't very clever about hiding what was going on. Only Dad hadn't guessed. And when he did find out, his whole world collapsed.'

She sipped her tea and then went on: 'I find it hard to forgive Mother for that. But let me tell you this, Dr Slater: if that lawyer is suggesting that Mother had something to do with Dad's death, then it's a lie.'

'Do you think Chris really saw her in the village that night?'

'Yes. He wouldn't say so unless he was sure, especially on oath.'

'Then why does your mother deny it?'

'I can't imagine. But you can take it from me she wasn't down in Uncle Lionel's cottage firing guns. Mother can be an exasperating person, but she'd never do anything violent.'

It had been a dull day, with only fleeting glimpses of the sun. Now, suddenly, it burst through the clouds and sent a shaft of brilliant light through the window on to the chair where Anne sat. I was shocked to see how tense and unhappy she looked.

'What's wrong between Chris and you, Anne?' I asked. She took a long time to answer. Then she said:

'I honestly don't know. Chris just says it's impossible for us to marry.'

'When did he tell you this?'

'Well, he actually told me the day after he came back from his holiday in Wales. But it started before then. It started the night Dad disappeared. Chris was in a queer mood right from the moment I met him at the station. You remember the way he behaved that evening?'

I remembered. He had been on edge and had nearly come to blows with Philip Brent over some trivial remark of Philip's.

We had finished our tea and were smoking cigarettes. I noticed that Anne, uncharacteristically, was taking quick, nervous puffs and tapping non-existent ash into an ashtray.

'I'm worried, Dr Slater,' she said. 'Durrand's got it in for Chris.'

'What do you mean?'

'Well, these questions in court today about the train Chris travelled on and about what he was doing before he left London—Durrand was behind that. I saw him scribble a note and pass it to one of the lawyers. Chris is hiding something and Durrand's on to it. I tell you I'm worried.'

I asked her if she was still seeing Chris. She shook her head miserably.

'He thinks it's better we shouldn't. Yet he still loves me. I know he does.'

The telephone rang. From the eager way Anne jumped up and went out to answer it I guessed she was hoping it might be Chris.

She was back in a couple of minutes, a wry grin on her face.

'An unexpected dinner invitation for tonight,' she said. 'From Owen Stryker, of all people.'

I remembered Jane's remarks.

'Your sister told me Stryker's been pestering you.'

'He's got a roving eye. He fancies his chance with anything in skirts under the age of twenty. But I can handle him. He's not a bad sort, really.'

'Did you accept?'

'Accept! Oh! I see—the dinner date. Yes, why not? Actually, he's got a legitimate excuse. He's just read the manuscript of my first novel and he wants to discuss it.'

It didn't surprise me that Anne wanted to write. She had many of the qualities of her father, energy, determination, perceptiveness and a feeling for language. I doubted, though, if she had Geoffrey's supreme conceit and self-confidence, which were in some ways his greatest assets.

'Yes,' Anne was going on, 'I don't mind Owen Stryker. And he knows his job. Of course, it was Dad that put him into the publishing business. Owen doesn't like to be reminded of that now, though.'

'I didn't know that.'

'Oh! yes. There was something discreditable about it. I don't know the story.'

CHAPTER 7

I took Philip Brent with me to Scotland. We left from King's Cross the third morning of the trial, when the prosecution had asked for an adjournment. It was clear we wouldn't be wanted to give evidence for some time.

I was glad to get away from Garston. I was out of favour with Julia, who appeared to hold me responsible for the evidence Chris had given.

Brent, too, was unpopular and he now explained to me why: Julia had guessed that it was he who had overheard her quarrel with Geoffrey and passed on the information to Lionel's lawyers.

'And did you?' I asked.

'Oh! yes. I passed their bedroom door about half past eleven that night and they were going at it hammer and tongs. Mrs Wallis was screaming at him.'

He didn't stand outside long enough to pick up what the quarrel was about. What he did hear was Julia's threat — 'If I thought you were really going to do that, Geoffrey, I'd put a bullet in you first.' 'She meant it, too,' Brent added.

'You said you were to be a witness at Court. Why weren't you called?'

Brent shrugged. 'Hocking decided to hold me back till later in the trial.'

His tone revealed his disappointment. No doubt he had been looking forward to being the central figure in a courtroom drama.

'And that's the extent of your evidence — the quarrel between Julia and Geoffrey?'

'No. More than that. I can confirm that Mrs Wallis was out on the afternoon of the murder.'

I had vaguely wondered where Brent himself had been that afternoon, for I hadn't seen him between lunch and dinner. Now he told me. Since Geoffrey had said he wouldn't need him, he had settled in a shady spot on the lawn behind the house and had lain there all afternoon alternately reading and dozing. Soon after six o'clock he heard a car go down the drive, followed, a minute or two later, by another. The first, he assumed, would be Geof-

frey's and the second Anne's. As he was going back into
the house just before seven, he noticed Mrs Wallis cycling
up the path towards the back gate. A moment or two
later he heard Anne's car pull up outside the front door.

'So you see,' he ended, 'the time agrees with what your
son said.'

'Philip,' I said, 'why do you sound so pleased about
this? Do you *want* to believe that Mrs Wallis had
something to do with her husband's death?'

Although he sulkily denied it, I knew it was true. Brent
had hero-worshipped Geoffrey and he had a violent an-
tipathy to the wife who had deceived him.

'And another thing,' I went on, 'how on earth could she
have done it? Is she supposed to have followed Geoffrey
on her bicycle to the cottage and shot him while Lionel
looked on? Then Lionel, I presume, kindly offers to wipe
her prints off the gun and put his own on instead? The
thing's preposterous.'

Brent was still sulky.

'Preposterous or not, Lionel's lawyers really believe she
did it. When old Mr Pearce interviewed me, I could tell
he thinks Mrs Wallis is guilty. They've some evidence we
don't know about yet. And besides, there's the glasses.'

'What about the glasses?'

'Why was there whisky and soda in both glasses? Lionel
Wallis never took soda in his whisky. He always had it
neat.'

I had seen that point myself and I wasn't much impressed
by it. How could one be sure that Lionel *never* took soda?
But now the significance of another piece of evidence
about these glasses came through to me. We were supposed
to believe that when Geoffrey called at his brother's cottage they had started by having a drink together.
Presumably Lionel would produce the bottle and glasses
and therefore you would expect to find his fingerprints on
both glasses. But they were only on one.

That was when I experienced the first twinge of doubt about Lionel's guilt.

The rain was teeming down as we emerged from our hotel in Glasgow next morning—a soft, relentless rain that held out no hope of improvement. The sky was yellowish-grey and it was as dark as a morning in November.

Cartshaw is some miles out of Glasgow to the south-east, in the heart of industrial Lanarkshire. Iron and steel are its lifeblood. Although prosperous enough today, in the black years of the depression it was hard hit; and memories in Cartshaw are long. Regardless of political trends elsewhere, an election in Cartshaw is a formality: the Socialist is unfailingly returned with a crushing majority.

All this we learned from an affable bus conductor. We were almost his only passengers, for at this time of day the traffic was mostly the other way, towards the city. I asked him about the pharmacy Lionel's uncle had had. He knew the shop and could tell us that it had been taken over by a multiple drug store. But he hadn't known Lionel, or his uncle.

It was a big shop, strategically sited in the heart of the shopping centre. Already whatever individuality it may have possessed had been welded into the stereotype set by its new owners.

I spoke briefly to the manager, a youngish man who had been transferred to Cartshaw from another branch. He knew nothing of the previous owner, nor did any of his staff, who had all been recruited since he took over. He gave us, however, the address of the solicitors who had acted for the seller.

Messrs Wainwright and Ross, Solicitors and Notaries Public, occupied a dim and cheerless suite of rooms above a bank, all dark-stained wood and dusty files. James Ross, the senior partner, who received us, might have stepped straight out of the *Forsyte Saga*, a thin, greying, precise little man in dark coat, white shirt and grey bow tie, pince-nez hanging from his ear. The Scots accent was somehow a shock. So too was the penetrating interrogation of our credentials.

When he had satisfied himself that we weren't from the press, he unbent a little. He admitted that he had known both Lionel and his uncle.

'Was Lionel always a drunkard?' Philip Brent asked out of the blue.

It had been a mistake to bring Brent here. I had already observed the look of distaste Ross had directed at him when he first came in. He was at his worst today, his duffle-coat fastened up to his chin, his beard wet from the rain; and he needed a haircut.

And now this brash question.

Ross froze. He remained polite, but he would tell us nothing. Only when I pressed him did he admit that the housekeeper who had looked after Lionel and his uncle still lived in the town, and reluctantly he gave me her address.

To avoid a repetition of that fiasco, I suggested to Brent that while I called on the housekeeper, he should scout around the town to see what he could pick up about the Wallis family.

Mrs McCreadie lived alone in an attic apartment in the industrial part of the town. Her wrinkled face had the withdrawn look of the very old. She was so deaf, too, that it was hard to communicate with her.

She was willing enough, however, to talk about Lionel and his uncle, whom she had served for many years. She launched into a series of rambling anecdotes, for the most part unintelligible to me because of the broad dialect in which they were told. All that emerged was her devoted loyalty to both Lionel and his uncle.

I was wondering how I could without rudeness stem the

flow, when the phrase 'terrible tragedy' penetrated to
me.

'Of course, that brother of Mr Lionel's was at the back
o' it. He cleared out as soon as it happened. That was
near thirty year ago and we never seen hide nor hair of
him since.'

'What happened?' I shouted at her.

But she ignored the question.

'Ah! poor Mr Lionel was never the same after it,' she
continued. And she was off on a new tack.

Try as I might, I couldn't get through to her. She was
less lucid now and her voice was tired. Suddenly her eyes
closed and she was asleep in her chair.

When I got to the Commercial Hotel, where we had arranged to meet, Philip Brent was already there. He was
excited.

'Never mind lunch just now,' he said. 'I've something to
show you in the library. We've just time before it closes at
one.'

He had taken my arm and was almost pulling me along
the street.

Presently we were in the reading room of the Cartshaw
Public Library, a huge bound volume of the *Cartshaw
Telegraph* open on a table in front of us.

'It's a weekly,' Brent was explaining as he flicked over
the pages. 'This is the second volume for 1936. I skimmed
through every issue for June and July that year and I
spotted — ah! there it is.'

He pointed to a column in the middle page of the issue
dated 10th July 1936. I read:

'LOCAL GIRL'S TRAGIC DEATH

'It is with deep regreat that we record the sudden pass-
ing of Miss Freda Harvey (22), second daughter of Dr
John Harvey, the prominent Cartshaw physician. Miss
Harvey was found dead in her bed last Saturday morn-

ing. An autopsy showed that she had died of an overdose of a barbiturate.

'At the Fatal Accidents Inquiry on Tuesday, after
hearing medical and other evidence, it was found that
Miss Harvey had taken her life while the balance of her
mind was disturbed.

'Miss Harvey was engaged to Mr Lionel Wallis,
nephew and business associate of Mr Peter Wallis, the
local chemist. They were to have been married in the
autumn.'

'That's a turn-up for the book, eh?' said Brent, smack-
ing his lips. 'I've worked it out: she died on the 4th, and
that's just about when Geoffrey would be here, isn't it? It
can't be just coincidence, can it?'

'I don't know,' I said shortly. I had suddenly lost taste
for the whole investigation. That yellowing page of
newspaper with its bald tale of tragedy of a generation
ago was a warning that I might be stirring up a hornets'
nest. But I was committed.

The one piece of positive information I had gleaned
from Mrs McCreadie was the address at which Lionel and
his uncle had lived. We went there, Brent and I, after
lunch.

'Well, well,' said Brent, when we saw it, 'the old boy
must have had money.'

It was a big house, certainly, solidly built, rather impressive in the uncompromising harshness of its lines. Just
now it was unoccupied and building materials were lying
about the garden. There was scaffolding against one side
of the house and workmen were knocking a great hole in
the gable.

A passer-by was sociable.

'They're making it into flats,' he remarked, as he saw us
looking in through the gate. 'It's far too big for one family
nowadays. It used to belong to Wallis—you know, the
murderer.'

Disappointed, perhaps, by our lack of surprise, he added: 'I knew him.'

'Who, Lionel Wallis?'

'Yes. Well, I really knew his uncle better. Very quiet chap, Lionel. But still waters, you know . . .'

When I pursued this, it turned out he had only a nodding acquaintance with Lionel Wallis and could tell me little about him.

'What friends did he have?' I asked.

'Don't think he had any. Very retiring sort of chap. Wait a minute, though, there's that lawyer fellow—what was his name? Little cock sparrow . . .'

'Ross?' I suggested.

'Yes, James Ross. He used to visit Lionel Wallis, I believe.'

This confirmed what I had suspected—that Ross knew more about Lionel than he had told us.

When the stranger had moved off, I said to Brent:

'I'm going back to see Ross, Philip.'

'Do you want me to come?'

'I'd rather go alone, if you don't mind.'

He stared at me, his face darkening. Then, without a word he turned on his heel and strode off. I cursed myself for not handling him more tactfully.

I was shown into Ross's office at once: he might almost have been expecting me.

He was more friendly this time. He offered me a cigar, which I refused. He lit one himself.

'Glad you came back,' he said. 'I rather thought you might. After you left this morning I phoned a man I know in the History Department at Glasgow University. He says that if you're doing the biography of Geoffrey Wallis, it won't simply be a pot-boiler.'

He puffed at his cigar for some moments, gazing over my head. I waited.

At last he went on:

'I take it you want to present the complete man, warts and all?'

'Certainly.'

'Because I know of one nasty great wart that Geoffrey Wallis managed to hide from nearly everybody else.'

He fell silent again; and again I didn't prompt him. He had his own pace and he wouldn't be hurried.

'I've practised in Cartshaw forty years, and my father another twenty before that. And all that time the Wallises were our clients. Peter Wallis—that's Lionel's uncle—was my closest friend. He was a hard-headed business man, but absolutely straight. His younger brother—the father of the two boys—took to the bottle and drifted from one job to another. Peter helped him out once or twice, but he wasn't one to throw good money after bad and eventually he wrote him off as a bad debt.

'However, when the brother died, Peter felt it was his duty to bring up the family. He took Lionel into his own home and he'd have taken the other boy too if your parents hadn't wanted to adopt him.

'Lionel was fifteen when he came here and he had already left school. His uncle wanted him to go back to school and then on to University, because he was a bright enough boy, although not a flier like Geoffrey. But Lionel never had much ambition. He preferred to go straight into his uncle's shop. He studied for the pharmaceutical exams and qualified as a chemist.

'When he became engaged to John Harvey's younger daughter, his uncle was delighted, for the Harveys were a nice family and Freda was a real bonny girl.

'Meanwhile Geoffrey was a student at Manchester and he used to spend part of his vacations in Cartshaw . . .'

Ross's story had the inevitability of a Greek tragedy. At Easter 1936, when Geoffrey visited his uncle's house, Lionel was in bed with influenza and he asked Geoffrey to take Freda around. Geoffrey needed no second invitation.

He set himself to captivate her and he took her by storm. His brilliance and charm made his brother seem pedestrian by comparison: the poor girl succumbed with scarcely a struggle. Lionel noticed nothing; only his uncle was suspicious.

When Freda found some weeks later that she was pregnant, she wrote to Geoffrey about it but still kept up the pretence with Lionel that everything was as before. Geoffrey stalled her with vague reassurances, but he was tired of the affair, and when he came to Cartshaw at the beginning of July he went to Freda and told her bluntly he was having nothing more to do with her and would deny responsibility for the baby. That same night Freda took an overdose of sleeping tablets.

It now came out, of course, that she had been pregnant, but only Peter Wallis guessed that Geoffrey had been responsible. He tackled him with it and Geoffrey admitted it. His uncle made him sign a confession and also exacted an undertaking that he would leave the country within a week and stay abroad until Lionel had got over the shock. If he didn't, his part in the affair would be made public.

According to Ross, Peter Wallis kept silent about what he knew, not for the sake of the family name, but to shield Lionel from the humiliation of knowing that his fiancée had been seduced by his own brother. Better that Lionel himself should be suspected (as, indeed, he was) of having anticipated marriage.

Only to his trusted friend Ross did Peter Wallis confide his secret. And Ross told no one.

'So Lionel never found out?' I asked.

Ross sighed.

'The mistake Peter made,' he said, 'was to hold on to that confession, imagining that he'd live for ever. He kept it in his safe at home. And then, of course, he went out like a light last October and hadn't time to destroy it.

Lionel found it in the safe after his uncle's death.'

When he found the confession, Lionel had gone to Ross for advice. Ross advised him to tear it up and put it out of his mind. No good could come of opening old wounds.

'He didn't take my advice, of course. In fact, he didn't really want it: his mind was already made up. He was determined to make his brother pay for what he'd done.'

'In other words, blackmail him?'

Ross hesitated. 'Well, not in the normal sense. Lionel's not interested in money. What he got from selling the shop would keep him in comfort for the rest of his days. No, it wasn't money he wanted from Geoffrey—he just wanted to see him suffer.'

So Lionel had disposed of his house and shop and descended without warning on his brother at Garston.

'That would be last Christmas?' I asked.

'Yes, Christmas Eve. He told Geoffrey he proposed to settle in his house, and that was that.'

'Why should Geoffrey be afraid of him? He hadn't committed a crime. Supposing Lionel *had* handed that confession to the police, they wouldn't have been interested.'

'That wasn't his idea at all. Lionel was threatening to send photostat copies to the press and to Geoffrey's friends and acquaintances.'

I could see how that would worry Geoffrey, who as the years passed prized respectability more and more and who was forever preaching sermons on the lowering of moral standards in this country. If he didn't actually say so, he implied that his own life had been a model of rectitude.

'Yes,' Ross went on, 'it was an effective enough threat. That's why Lionel was able to stay at Garston so long I got one or two letters from him. He was making Geoffrey squirm, dropping hints every now and again and when other people were there, but never actually letting the cat right out of the bag.'

'He must really have hated Geoffrey, to go to these lengths.'

'Oh! he hated him all right. Hated him enough to kill him, I'd have said, except . . .'

'Yes?'

'Well, except that he's not that kind of man.'

Lionel to me was a shadowy figure. On the one occasion I myself had met him his personality had made almost no impression. I asked Ross about him now.

'There's always been something naive and trusting about Lionel,' he said. 'He's honest himself and it seldom crosses his mind that others might be less so. The way he lost his fiancée to Geoffrey was typical. Of course, the great tragedy of his life was when Freda died. He was never the same after that. He'd always been a lonely bird, but he became practically a recluse. He didn't keep very well, either—used to have blackouts occasionally. And, to be honest, he drank more than was good for him, especially in recent years. I used to jolly him along—I got him interested in stamps—but it was hard going. I can't pretend he was lively company.'

'Do the police know about Freda Harvey?' I asked.

'You mean, do they know about Geoffrey being involved? I doubt it. They certainly didn't get it from me, though they've been up here snooping. They've a strong enough case against Lionel already without me handing them a motive on a plate.'

'You don't believe he's guilty, then?'

The little man glared fiercely at me.

'I don't *want* to believe he's guilty.'

CHAPTER 8

When I returned south, I had one more week of preparation before I started writing. Philip Brent had arranged interviews for me with people who had known Geoffrey Wallis at various stages in his career. Again and again I heard the same verdict: a real craftsman whose work commanded respect, but a cold, self-centred, ambitious man. And this despite his popularity with the masses as a television personality; for the image he projected on the screen was synthetic and false.

I asked those I interviewed if Geoffrey had ever spoken of the two years he had spent on the continent just before the last war. It didn't suprise me that the answer was 'No'.

My last appointment was with Owen Stryker. I began by telling him what I had learned in Scotland. I had the odd impression that Stryker knew it all already.

'Well done, Professor,' was his only comment when I had finished. 'And now that you've solved that mystery, I take it you're ready to—'

'I've learned why Geoffrey went abroad, not what he did there. I can't write a man's biography when two years of his life are a total blank.'

We were in the London offices of Harrington and Leigh. Stryker's room was untidy, the desk littered with papers, and on the floor a sprawling heap of manuscripts.

He was showing signs of irritation.

'Look here, Slater,' he said, 'you must get on with this job. It's not a thesis you're writing—you don't have to account for every time Wallis brushed his teeth.'

'He could have brushed his teeth a few times in two years,' I remarked.

Stryker glared at me. Then he seemed to come to a decision.

'As a matter of fact,' he said, 'there's no mystery. Geoffrey knocked around Paris for a year. Kept himself from starving by giving English lessons, and he also took odd jobs in hotels and cafés—washing dishes, that sort of thing. When he'd saved enough he retired to the Tyrol to write his first novel.'

'He told you this himself?'

'Yes.'

'Well, that's a start, anyway. I may go over to Paris myself to see if I can fill in the gaps.'

This time I could almost feel the drop in temperature.

'I shouldn't do that if I were you,' he said coldly.

'Why not?'

'There isn't time.'

As if the matter were settled, Stryker abruptly changed the subject.

'Do you know,' he said, indicating the pile of manuscripts on the floor, 'that there's something like a million words here waiting to be read? And most of it tripe. Far too many people think they can write. It's all this education.'

'What took you into publishing?' I asked, remembering Anne's remark. 'Didn't Geoffrey Wallis have something to do with it?'

He eyed me narrowly.

'I wonder where you got that idea,' he said lightly.

It was now well into September. Even Philip Brent, who approved my painstaking research, was becoming anxious.

Stryker had said he must have the manuscript by the end of October. That had given me seven weeks; five weeks really, for term started in the middle of October and I wouldn't have much free time after that.

The form of the book had been taking shape in my

mind over the past weeks. I knew roughly what I wanted
to say and how I wanted to say it. I had masses of material
on Geoffrey Wallis—his diaries and correspondence,
reviews of his books and plays, the books themselves, and
the voluminous notes I had made.

Two major problems remained. One was the manner
of Geoffrey's death: I had to get the facts of the murder
right. That would have to wait for the outcome of the
trial, which dragged on and on.

The other problem worried me more, the mystery sur-
rounding the two years Geoffrey had spent abroad.
Stryker's sketchy account was not only inadequate, it was
entirely unverified; besides, Geoffrey's own reticence
about it was significant and intriguing.

That could wait too, though not for long. In the mean-
time I was ready to start the early chapters.

On the first day I dictated nearly 10,000 words into
Geoffrey's tape recorder. These early chapters were easy
to write, for they dealt with events of which I had first-
hand knowledge. I was back in my boyhood again, but
seeing Geoffrey now through adult eyes. I liked him even
less in retrospect. As I dictated, I was bringing out—
almost without willing it—his selfishness, his ingratitude
for all that my parents had done for him.

'Was Daddy really as awful as that?'

The voice startled me. I had been so engrossed that I
hadn't heard the study door open behind me.

Jane had returned to Garston the previous week. I had
seen little of her, for she had taken up again with the boy
on the motorcycle.

'Where's Tony today?' I asked her, not pleased by the
interruption.

She made a face. 'He's gone off with his Pop to some
ghastly place in Yorkshire on a fishing trip. Just my
luck—as soon as I get back, away he goes.'

'Hadn't you better switch that thing off?' she added,

pointing to the tape recorder. 'You don't want Trotsky typing our conversation, do you?'

'Trotsky?'

'Phil Brent. That's what Anne christened him. The beard, you know, and the accent.'

I clicked off the machine. She heard my sigh.

'Oh! I'm holding you back,' she exclaimed, all remorse, and turned to go.

But my concentration was broken and I felt the need to relax. Besides, there was something rather appealing about Jane.

'No, don't go,' I said. 'Talk to me about your father. You asked if he was really as bad as I make him out. What did you think of him?'

She sat down now, and rested her chin on her hand, a self-conscious pose expressing concentrated thought.

'It's a funny thing,' she said, 'but I hardly knew Daddy. Of course, I was away at school a lot, but he had no time for me even when I was here. Anne was always his favourite. I don't mean he was unkind. But he never talked to me the way he talked to Anne. He resented me for being a girl. He wanted a son, you see.'

That at least was true. In an unguarded moment Geoffrey had once admitted to me his bitter disappointment that he had never had a son.

'The only two people he really cared for,' Jane went on, 'were Mummy and Anne. And latterly, of course, poor Mummy was in the doghouse . . . What do you think of the co-respondent — Durrand, I mean?'

Another of Anne's nicknames, I guessed.

She answered her own question: 'He's the original square. Mummy must be getting senile to have fallen for him. Of course, everybody knows what *he's* after. It's the money. Anne says he's broke.'

As she prattled on, my attention began to wander: I was anxious to get back to work, for the next chapter was building up in my mind. Later I had cause to regret my inattention.

'. . . in the dustbin, so I pulled them out. The pages were torn, but I managed to fit them together like a jig-saw. It's hot stuff and some people wouldn't like it if they knew I'd read it. What do you think I ought to do, Dr Slater?'

'Sorry, Jane, I didn't quite follow all that. What did you—'

'You weren't listening,' she said, with hurt dignity, and turned towards the door.

Even then I might have persuaded her to repeat her story, if Philip Brent hadn't chosen that moment to burst in.

He had started to transcribe the first of the tapes and he was full of enthusiasm.

'It's marvellous,' he said, 'just marvellous. I simply had to come and tell you. If you can keep this up—oh! it's marvellous!'

'Just marvellous,' mimicked Jane, as she minced out, her head in the air.

Although I never again approached the output of that first day, I made steady progress, and Philip was stretched to keep the typing up-to-date.

Julia took an anxious interest in the book's develop-ment. Rather than wait for Philip's typescript she would play back the day's recordings each evening. She never criticized, not even the more flamboyant passages of which I was myself ashamed and which the blue pencil put right when I got the typed sheets from Philip.

Her attitude to me at this time was puzzling. She was ill at ease, and avoided, when she could, being alone with me. When she did speak to me, it was with an apologetic, guilty air that should have warned me. But I was too wrapped up in my writing.

One evening, when I was in the study revising the typescript, Arthur Durrand came in. It had been a hot, windless day and even now, with the sun dipping low in the west and the light beginning to fade, I had the windows thrown wide and was still too warm.

Durrand was feeling the heat too, I noticed, as he eased himself into a chair with the exaggerated care of the stout man. He was wearing an off-white linen suit and brown tie. Even in casual wear like that he contrived to look over-dressed.

'I just looked in,' he said, 'to compliment you on the book. It's going splendidly.'

I was annoyed. Although I had allowed Julia to play back the tapes, I hadn't expected her to invite an audience.

He ignored my frown.

'I notice,' he remarked, 'that you've skipped the couple of years Geoffrey was abroad.'

Julia had made the same remark the previous day. I gave Durrand the answer I had given her.

'I'm coming back to it later. I've still some research to do.'

'You should talk to Owen Stryker. He's got all the dope about it.'

'I've talked to Stryker and I've drafted a few paragraphs from what he told me. But I'm not satisfied. I'm going across to Paris myself to see if I can pick up the trail from there.'

Durrand took off his spectacles and began to polish them.

'I'd rather you didn't,' he said mildly, his eyes blinking myopically.

This was why he had come tonight, I guessed. Julia had sent him, no doubt.

For the moment he changed the subject. 'Did you know

that Lionel Wallis takes blackouts?'

'I did hear that, yes. Why?'

'It was news to me, I must say. But look at this.'

Taking an envelope from his breast pocket, he extracted a foolscap sheet and handed it to me.

'What is it?' I asked.

'It's a copy of Lionel's statement to his solicitors. This is what his defence is based on.'

'How did you get it?'

'Never mind how I got it. I have my contacts. You can take it from me it's genuine. Read it.'

I switched on the table lamp.

'My brother made an appointment' (I read) 'to see me at 6.15 on 28th July. I knew why he was coming. He wanted to recover a certain document which I held, and I knew he would try to bribe me and perhaps also threaten me.

'Mr Stryker called about 4 o'clock. I had a few drinks with him but was not drunk. We talked about various matters. He left just before 6 o'clock. I washed the glasses we had been using and put them away. My brother arrived at 6.15 and parked his car outside the gate.

He seemed nervous. He asked if he could have a drink. I got out two glasses and poured a whisky and soda for my brother and a whisky for myself. What happened after that I do not know. My memory is blank.

'When I woke it was dark. I was lying on my back on the floor with something hard clutched in my right hand. There was a noise like the hiss of escaping gas. At first I did not know where I was. When I tried to get up I was dizzy and fell down again. I groped about on hands and knees searching for the door. I crawled over a cloth-covered object like a badly stuffed cushion. The cloth felt wet and sticky. When I found the door I pulled myself up and switched on the light. My brother lay in a pool of blood on the carpet. He was dead. It was his body I had crawled over. Everything in the room was smashed. I was still clutching the hard object in my right hand without comprehending what it was. It was a gun, it was my brother's gun. I recognized it, for he had threatened me with it once before, at Garston.

'I looked at my watch. It was 1.18 a.m. It was clear to me what had happened. There had been a struggle and I had somehow got my brother's gun away from him and shot him; and then I had fainted.

'I was still dizzy and unable to think clearly. My one idea was to escape. I opened the front door and threw the gun into the bushes. It was then I recognized that the hissing sound I had heard was rain. While I was standing at the door a flash of lightning lit up the hillside and I saw my brother's car standing outside the gate. That gave me the idea of how I might get far enough away before there was any hue and cry.

'I went through my brother's pockets for the ignition key. Then I dragged his body out of the house and forced it into the back of the car. It was very heavy. My clothes were covered with blood, so I changed into another suit and put the bloodstained suit in the back of the car beside the body. I drove round by the river and bypassed the village. I turned north at . . .'

(There followed a detailed account of Lionel's journey to Aberlandry, the disposal of the body and the bloodstained clothes there, and his subsequent travels, culminating in his arrest in Liverpool.)

'I made a statement to the police when I was arrested. I admitted that I must have shot my brother, although I did not remember it. I said that it must have been in self-defence after a struggle, since my brother had brought the gun with him.

'At that time I believed I had shot my brother I do not believe it now. I have been told that dregs of whisky and soda were found in my glass. I never take soda with

whisky; someone must have tampered with the glass. Also
the blackout is very strange. I have a mild heart condition
which sometimes causes me to lose consciousness briefly.
My doctor in Cartshaw can testify to it. But these blackouts are for a minute, two minutes, once ten minutes—
never seven hours.

'If anyone says I have acted as only a guilty man would
act, he does not know the meaning of the word panic.'

'What do you think of it?' asked Durrand.

'The language is very stiff. Lionel doesn't really talk
like that, surely.'

'Oh! they doctor it up. "Do not" for "don't" and so on.
But it wasn't the style I was asking about—it was the content. Do you believe Lionel's story?'

'I suppose not. It's so implausible, and yet—I don't
know, there's something impressive about it.'

Durrand eyed me speculatively.

'Well, I can tell you this. The police are half convinced.
They're re-opening the whole case.'

It was almost dark outside. Durrand's chair was beyond
the pool of light from the little lamp on the table and his
face was in shadow. Only his voice betrayed his nervousness.

'I'm going to put my cards on the table, Maurice,' he
said. 'Julia and I—well, you know how it is between us,
you're not blind. Some day, when all this has died down,
we hope to get married. I've got a favour to ask and it's for
Julia that I'm asking it. You see, the police have been
questioning her again after what came out at Court. She's
terribly upset. I don't blame Chris so much as that young
ass, Brent. Why Julia allows him to stay under her roof
after what he did is beyond me . . .'

'All right,' I interrupted, 'Julia's worried. What am I
supposed to do?'

Still he was reluctant to come to the point.

'You're not seriously thinking of going abroad to dig up Geoffrey's past, are you?'

'Yes, I am.'

'Don't do it, Maurice. I beg of you, for Julia's sake don't do it.'

'Why on earth not?'

'Stryker can tell you all you need. He knows more about that period of Geoffrey's life than anyone else. The one thing Stryker doesn't know isn't really relevant for your purpose. It's something that could do Julia great harm if it came out.'

I was beginning to get his drift.

'You mean it would give her a motive for Geoffrey's murder?'

'Ah! Maurice, how quick you are! Yes, I mean precisely that. And since we both know that Julia did not murder her husband, we must spare her that anxiety. Because if you go careering off to Austria at this stage, you can be sure the police will make it their business to find out what you learned there.'

At least I had discovered now that the secret lay in Austria and not in France.

'I'm sorry, Arthur,' I said shortly. 'I couldn't possibly make any such promise. I'm writing Geoffrey's biography and I'll do it in my own way.'

'It was Julia who got you that contract, you know. It could be cancelled.'

'Not by Julia. My contract is with Harrington and Leigh.'

The velvet glove was now peeled off.

'If Lionel's innocent, Julia isn't the only candidate for his place in the dock. Spare a thought for Chris. If you value your son, Maurice, you'll think over what I've said.'

He had gone out before I could reply.

CHAPTER 9

Three days after Durrand's visit Superintendent Caswell came to Garston. I saw him arrive just after lunch, but it was nearly four o'clock when he knocked on the study door.

'Mrs Wallis said I'd find you here. May I disturb you?'

The study was littered with the raw material of the biography—Geoffrey's books, his diaries, my own notes and reference works. I had to clear come of the typescript off a chair to let Caswell sit down.

'How's it going?' he asked, glancing round with interest.

'I'm waiting for you chaps to write the last chapter for me,' I answered lightly.

He wasn't amused. Caswell was a tall, spare man, in physique and demeanour not unlike the laconic, unsmiling hero of an old-time Western. I had thought that humour lurked in his quiet grey eyes, but there was none. He seemed to have an obsessive devotion to duty.

'I talked to your son yesterday,' he said now.

'Oh! yes?'

'He wasn't very co-operative. Foolish of him.'

Before Caswell could go on, there was a chink of crockery and the door burst open. Jane marched in backwards, bearing a tray with tea. She thumped it down unceremoniously on the hearthrug.

'Mummy told me to bring it,' she mumbled ungraciously.

'That was kind of her,' said Caswell.

Jane rounded on him. She was dramatizing the situation as usual; but I think she was genuinely angry too.

'It's more than you deserve, after the way you gave her the third degree. Mummy was in tears just now, yes, in *tears*. You're just a great big bully.' She slammed the door behind her.

When she had gone, Caswell remarked stiffly:

'I need hardly say that Miss Wallis is misrepresenting what happened. My conversation with her mother was perfectly amicable.

'It did last, though, for nearly two hours.'

'We had a lot of ground to cover.'

Caswell had been put out of his stride. I took the chance to slip in a question of my own.

'Does this mean the case is being re-opened?'

'It's never been closed. Just because somebody's been arrested doesn't mean we're through. There are always loose ends to be tied up . . . And, of course, occasionally, just occasionally, something turns up to make us change our minds. We're not vindictive, you know; all we want to get at is the truth. If we've made a mistake, we'll admit it.'

'And you think you've made a mistake here?'

Caswell didn't answer immediately. He bent down and lifted the tray and put it on the desk on top of the papers. With deft movements he set out the cups and saucers and began to pour out.

He spoke without looking up:

'A doubt has been raised, a serious doubt. It wouldn't be proper for me to say more than that.'

He busied himself with the civilities of handing my tea and offering plates. The practised way he did it suggested the family man.

'We were speaking of your son, Dr Slater,' he said, when he had settled again. 'Do you know where he was on the afternoon of the day Mr Wallis was murdered?'

'He was on duty. He said so himself in court.'

'Yes. Unfortunately his employers don't corroborate it. They say he had the afternoon off.'

I felt a stab of irritation with Chris. It was so unlike him to be untruthful. Why did he have to tell such a stupid, pointless lie?

'Geoffrey Wallis wasn't murdered in the afternoon.' I pointed out. 'He was alive at 6.15.'

'There's a train from London that reaches Minford at 5.35 —'

'What of it? Chris was on the later train. Anne met him at the station. 6.42, it gets in.'

Caswell nodded. 'Miss Wallis met him at the station. But that's no proof that he got off that train. In fact, there's some evidence the other way. He said in court, you remember, that it was an express and that Minford was the first stop. He was specifically asked if it had stopped anywhere that night. He said "No".'

Caswell carefully stirred his tea.

'We happen to know,' he continued, 'that it did stop that night. At Clovering Halt, the little station that serves Sir John Cressey's place. They stop there on request. Lady Cressey was on the train that night and it stopped at Clovering to let her off. That's why it was a minute or two late at Minford.'

The first prickle of alarm was running down my spine.

'And how is Chris supposed to have got to the cottage and back?' I asked. 'It's all of six miles from Minford station.'

'Not by the back way. It's suggested that he borrowed a bicycle — there are always railway workers' cycles parked in the yard behind the station. He could have taken the short cut by the track over the fields and across the river. It's less than two miles. He could easily have been back before the next train got in. A man was seen cycling down that track just after six o'clock.'

'You say "it's suggested". Who suggests it?'

The superintendent didn't answer. He was stolidly munching a biscuit.

'And another thing,' I went on angrily, 'how could

Chris possibly know that Geoffrey would be at his brother's cottage at that time and that he would have obligingly brought his gun for Chris to shoot him with?'

'As far as the revolver's concerned, the answer might be that your son — or, let's say, the murderer — took it to the cottage, not Wallis himself.'

'You mean, the murderer had removed it from Garston some time before?'

'Yes. It wouldn't be difficult. It was kept in that drawer there, unlocked,' He was pointing at the upper left-hand drawer of Geoffrey's desk. Mechanically I opened it: it was empty.

Caswell went on to explain how the murder might have been done. He was careful to point out that his explanation depended on the hypothesis, which as yet he didn't accept, that Lionel was innocent.

'Geoffrey Wallis,' he said, 'was desperate to recover a certain document which his brother held. We know what it was, by the way; we found it among Lionel Wallis's papers in the cottage.'

'It concerned the girl Harvey, didn't it?' I interrupted. 'A confession by Geoffrey that he'd been responsible for her suicide?'

'Oh! you know about that, do you?' The superintendent was taken aback. 'Yes, that was it. The girl had been engaged to Lionel, apparently . . . Anyway, Geoffrey formed a plan to get it back. He called by arrangement at his brother's cottage, he asked for a drink, and he slipped something into Lionel's glass. While Lionel was out for the count, Geoffrey had leisure to search the cottage for the confession . . . Only it didn't work out like that. You see, somebody else knew of Geoffrey's plan.'

He broke off. He was eyeing me closely.

'You told me that,' he added unexpectedly.

'*I* did? When?'

Caswell took a paper from his pocket.

'I brought this along from the Yard,' he said. 'It's the statement you made the day after Wallis's body was found.'

He had put on a pair of American-style rimless spectacles and he skimmed through the sheets until he found the place he wanted.

'Uh-huh. Here we are: "The day after he got back from London he took me out in this car." (That's the 26th—two days before his death.) "His manner was strange. He said he was going to do something that would cause his family much distress. I asked him jokingly if he was going to commit a murder. He said—and I do not think he was joking—that he had considered that, but after taking advice he now had a better plan. He added that it was just a side issue." You remember that conversation, do you?'

'Yes.'

'Well, side issue or not, don't you think he was referring to his plan for dealing with Lionel?'

I agreed that that was plausible.

'There are two significant phrases in your statement. One of them is "*after taking advice*, he now had a better plan." '

'You mean it implies that somebody else knew the plan?'

'Rather more than that. Somebody else *suggested* the plan to him. Now suppose this helpful planner—call him Mr X—turns up at the cottage when Stage 1 has been completed. Lionel is in a drugged sleep in his chair. Geoffrey has just begun his search. Mr X pumps lead into Geoffrey from the revolver he had previously removed from Garston. He takes the two glasses from the table and rinses them out (he has to do both of them because he isn't sure which is the one that was drugged) and then puts a little whisky and soda into each. He presses Lionel's fingers on one glass and Geoffrey's on the other and places the glasses on the mantelshelf. He forces the gun into Lionel's right hand. Then he knocks about the furniture to make it seem there's been a fight. And off he goes. Lionel is going to have his work cut out explaining all that when he wakes up. As it happens, he gets himself deeper into the mire by taking fright and running.'

Caswell's manner told me that this was no wild hypothesis. Despite his denials, he really believed that was what had happened, he no longer thought Lionel guilty.

'You said there were two significant phrases in my statement,' I reminded him. 'What was the other?'

'The fact that Geoffrey Wallis had just got back from London when he had that conversation with you. What was he doing in London? I suggest that's when he got the disastrous "advice".'

Caswell got up and went over to the window and stood with his back to me, looking out.

'We've been trying to trace his movements over these days,' he said. 'He was at Television House most of Sunday evening. On Monday he had business appointments with his lawyers and then his publishers. We don't know what he did during the day on Tuesday, but—' Caswell swung round and faced me—'he spent the whole of that evening alone with your son. They had dinner in Wallis's Club and afterwards retired to a private room.'

I kept the reins on my temper, for there was one thing more I wanted to find out.

'And what, may I ask, was Chris's motive for murdering Geoffrey Wallis?'

Caswell picked his words carefully.

'It's been suggested that Wallis was refusing his consent to the marriage. It's also been suggested that your son stood to gain financially, since his fiancée would come into a lot of money on her father's death.'

I couldn't contain myself any longer.

'What the hell d'you mean by "it's been suggested"? If

you think Chris is a murderer, say so—don't shelter behind somebody else.'

But the superintendent was unruffled.

'Dr Slater,' he said patiently, 'I came here today hoping you might help your son. When I say "it's been suggested", I mean exactly that. Somebody is giving us information against him. Frankly, I don't believe he's a murderer. But he's a damned fool. He won't answer questions. And there's quite a case for him to answer now. I hoped you might drive some sense into his head.'

I apologized. 'All right, superintendent, I'll speak to him.'

'You'll understand, of course,' Caswell added, 'that what I've been saying to you this afternoon is in strict confidence. As far as the public is concerned, we still have no doubt that Lionel Wallis is guilty.'

He put his glasses into a case and looked steadily at me. I could see that he had been indiscreet in telling me as much as he had. Now I learned why.

'In writing Wallis's biography,' he said, 'you're bound to learn things that we'd never discover. If you come across anything, anything at all, however insignificant it may seem, that could have some bearing on his death, let me know at once. You see, if the theory I've given you is correct, it's one of the most cold-blooded, devilish crimes on record; and one of the cleverest. We need all the help we can get.'

He turned towards the door, but then stopped.

'Another thing,' he said. 'Watch yourself. Be careful what you say to people. A man like our Mr X wouldn't hesitate to strike again.'

CHAPTER 10

I had a brief and unsatisfactory talk with Chris on the telephone that evening. When I advised him to be frank with the police, he said it was his business and he knew what he was doing. He made excuses when I suggested we should meet: he hadn't a free moment, it seemed.

Finally I asked about Anne: was he seeing her again? His only answer was to replace the receiver.

When Chris was younger, his relationship with me had gone through phases like that, when he seemed to despise and dislike me. Always the cause could be traced to his mother. Helen couldn't deprive me of my legal right to see Chris, but she did all in her power to make these occasions painful.

Although Helen's influence over Chris had weakened as he grew up and began to exercise an independent judgement, he had never entirely broken free. I wondered now whether Helen might once again have turned him against me.

Once the thought had come, it was an obsession. I hardly slept that night, and by the morning I had worked myself into a fury against Helen. I determined to have it out with her.

It was fifteen years since our marriage had broken up, twelve since I had seen her. My bank still sent her a cheque every month for twice as much as the alimony she had been awarded: I had started it for Chris's benefit and when he grew up and no longer needed the money I hadn't the heart to reduce the allowance.

I got regular news of Helen from Chris. It was natural for him to talk of his mother and I steeled myself to listen without betraying the disgust that her name evoked.

After she left me, she and Chris went to stay with her mother in Croydon. Helen inherited the house when the mother died, and she eked out her income by taking in paying guests. She was comfortably off; I had made it my business to find out.

The first separation from his mother came when Chris did his National Service; and after that he started a training which required him to live in the hotel. That had given me much satisfaction, for it showed that he was breaking away gradually from the apron strings. Or so I had thought.

The house was bigger than I had remembered: a pleasant two-storeyed building with a small garage attached. I had been in it once or twice in the early days of our marriage, when Helen's father was alive. I dimly remembered him as a large man with a crop of iron-grey hair whose main interest was the internal combustion engine. He had owned a garage somewhere in the East End.

My heart was pounding as I rang the bell. But the door was opened by an elderly, angular woman wearing a long tweed skirt and lace blouse.

'I'm afraid Mrs Slater is out,' she said. The voice was low and cultured. Faded gentility; one of the paying guests, no doubt.

'Who shall I say called?' she added. But I was already turning away, relieved that my impulsive urge to see Helen had been frustrated. My anger had evaporated and my only thought was to get away.

I was opening my car door when I saw her. She was crossing the street towards me, a trim figure in tight green skirt and jacket, saucy red hat, and stiletto heels. She walked past me unseeing and turned towards her gate.

'Helen!' I called involuntarily.

She stopped and peered at me. She had always been short-sighted but had refused to wear glasses.

'Well, well,' she said, 'this is a surprise, Maurice. It must be ten years since—'

'Twelve,' I corrected her.

We stood uncertainly on the pavement for a moment; then she invited me in.

The room she showed me into took my breath away. It had a royal blue fitted carpet and one of those incredibly expensive velvety wallpapers, maroon with a gold motif. The suite was covered in yellow moquette and the curtains too were a garish yellow.

It was hideous, especially as the setting for all the junk that Helen had gathered round her—fussy little tables, ornaments, pictures that had caught her undiscriminating eye at one time or another.

Helen herself was less brassy than I had expected: her hair, not dyed, but streaked with grey, her face lined and not heavily made-up. Although she had put on weight, her figure was still youthful enough for the close-fitting clothes to be provocative and not ridiculous. At 42 she still had more sex appeal than Julia ever had.

Geoffrey never understood why I had married Helen, who lacked all the qualities he regarded as indispensable in a wife. The answer was simple: it was wartime, I was young, Helen was beautiful.

'What'll you have, Maurice? I can't offer you whisky, I'm afraid, but—'

'Gin will do, gin and something.' I knew she'd have gin.

As she got the drinks, she asked me:

'Were you visiting me, Maurice, or did you just happen to be passing?'

Her manner was friendly, almost flirtatious. 'Almost'? It *was* flirtatious. It was the way she used to act with my friends to annoy and embarrass me. The recollection disgusted me.

'What lies have you been telling Chris about me?' I said baldly.

The smile froze on her face and her eyes took on the sullen look I remembered so well.

She lit a cigarette.

'When Chris got engaged to the Wallis girl,' she said jerkily, between puffs, 'I told him he was following in his daddy's footsteps. I said the girl's mother had been your mistress.

'You see,' she went on, 'all Chris knows is that I divorced you for adultery. I'd never put a name to the woman before, but now I told him it was Julia. He believed it. Mind you'—she laughed again—'Julia wouldn't have said no to a bit of byplay with you. She's the nympho type.'

It was no use losing my temper with her. Nor could I appeal to her better nature: she had none. I had allowed Helen to divorce me on manufactured evidence, although she was the one who had deserted me and who had had a series of squalid affairs. I had never let Chris know the truth about his mother, but I didn't expect, and certainly didn't get, any gratitude from her.

She seemed to sense what was going through my mind.

'You know, Maurice,' she said, 'you enjoy being a martyr. You like to feel superior and forgiving. You always did. And, by God, you were superior enough when we were married. I was common, I was dirt, you were ashamed of me. I wasn't good enough for your academic friends.'

She went over and poured herself another drink. Her hand was shaking.

'Look at this room,'—she waved her glass—'you think it's cheap, I saw the look in your face. Well, I *like* it. You never stopped to consider what I liked, did you? I liked dancing and the pictures and a bit of fun. But no, every night I had to sit twiddling my thumbs while you pored over your precious books. Every bloody night. Do you wonder I left you?

'I had Chris, though. You weren't going to get him. I've used every trick in the book to keep him and I'm not ashamed of it. I've slaved for him and I've brought him up decently and I'm not going to give him up now, even if I have to tell lies to keep him.'

She was sobbing. Against all reason she had got through my defences. For the very first time I was seeing her point of view, and recognizing that perhaps she had had some excuse for her boredom and her flirtations, even for her unfaithfulness. I hadn't tried very hard to adjust my way of life to hers.

'Helen,' I said now, as gently as I could, 'it's not for my sake that I'm asking you to take back these lies, it's for Chris. Anne's a nice girl and he's in love with her. You mustn't be possessive.'

'It's not that,' she replied distractedly. 'I don't mind him marrying, if it's the right girl. But not into that family. They're rotten. The mother's a queer fish and the father—well, you know what he was like. And then that other girl was in a mental home.'

'What other girl?'

'The sister—the younger sister.'

'What! Jane?'

'Yes. She had some kind of nervous breakdown.'

Helen was so unreliable that I had no idea whether to believe this or not.

A key turned in the lock of the front door.

Helen gave me a sardonic glance.

'That'll be Chris,' she said.

Chris stood in the doorway, blinking at the unfamiliar sight of his father and mother together.

'Join us for a drink, Chris,' said Helen, laughing harshly. 'This calls for a celebration.' She sounded slightly tipsy.

Chris ignored her.

'What are you doing here?' he said sharply to me. It was an accusation rather than a question.

If Helen had kept her mouth shut, I would have retired

defeated. I didn't want Chris to be a witness to sordid recriminations between his parents; that was a price I wasn't prepared to pay even to re-establish myself in his eyes.

So I made a non-committal reply and made towards the door. But Helen intervened. She was confident of her power over Chris and had to demonstrate it to me.

'Your father came here,' she said, 'to persuade me to take back what I said about him and Julia Wallis.'

'And did he persuade you?' asked Chris quietly.

I spotted it then, the odd little catch in his voice, the tension underlying his words. But Helen ignored the danger signals.

'Why should I?' she replied. 'It's true. Every word I said about them.'

'Really?' said Chris. 'My information is different. I've been asking questions this past week, questions I should have asked years ago. I know now why your marriage went on the rocks, Mother, and it's a very different story from the one I've been brought up on.'

His voice was harsh now and implacable, his face stony. Helen gazed at him in disbelief.

'What about Fred Stables?' he went on. 'And Eddie Carson? Do you remember them? And wasn't there a character called Gregor Smith?'

Chris had done his research thoroughly. These were the three men whose names had been linked with Helen's during our marriage.

'And all these years you've had me believing that—' the accusing voice pressed on inexorably.

'Stop it, Chris!' I shouted. Helen had collapsed into a chair and was sobbing uncontrollably, her hands covering her face.

Chris looked at me in surprise, as if he had forgotten I was there.

'But—'

'I said, stop it! Leave her now, you've said enough.'

He stood irresolute for a moment, then turned and went out.

'Helen?' I said gently, 'I'm sorry this has happened. But he'll be back. He—'

She took her hands away from her face and looked at me with hatred.

'Get the hell out of here,' she screamed. Her eyes were swollen and the tears were running down her cheeks.

Chris was standing beside the car when I came down. He made no demur when I told him to get in.

I hardly noticed where I drove, except that I headed south, away from the city. Chris sat hunched in the seat beside me, his face grim and brooding. Neither of us spoke.

Presently the traffic began to thin out, a splash of green appeared now and then between the houses; soon we were in the country.

I never did discover the name of the village where we had lunch. We reached it after meandering aimlessly through a maze of minor roads. It was just a cluster of houses and an inn.

We tried the inn. They didn't do lunches as a rule, we were told, but the landlord was pleased enough to heat soup for us and to provide bread and cheese. And tankards of beer. We had the room to ourselves.

I had always hoped that some day the scales would fall from Chris's eyes and he would see his mother for what she was. But now that it had happened, the moment had turned sour on me. I couldn't get Helen's ravaged face out of my mind.

'Don't be too hard on her, Chris,' I said. 'She couldn't help herself. It's for you that she did it. She couldn't bear to lose you.'

Chris went on eating his soup.

'You're all she's got, Chris,' I added. He looked up then, and my heart sank to see the hardness in his eyes.

'She should have thought of that when she lied to me,' he said.

Chris's code was a hard one, and rigid; it gave little weight to clemency and pity. Perhaps later, when he had got over the shock, he might be reconciled. But not yet.

'That's where you were that Saturday afternoon?' I asked him.

He nodded. 'I wanted to tell her of the engagement. It was my afternoon off and I went down for lunch.'

'Why didn't you take Anne with you?'

'I knew Mother would be upset. I thought it would be easier if I broke it to her myself. I'd been putting it off—it was nearly a fortnight since we'd got engaged.'

'How did she take it?'

'Very quietly—too quietly. Then after lunch she came out with that story about you and Mrs Wallis. Said she felt it was her duty to tell me.'

'And you believed her?'

I was taken aback by the vehemence of his answer: 'Of course I believed her. Ever since I was old enough to understand, it's been impressed on me that she divorced you for adultery. You never thought it worthwhile to tell me what really happened. Why shouldn't I believe that Mrs Wallis was the woman?'

'I didn't want to turn you against your mother. That's why I never spoke.'

His silence condemned me. Chris believed that the truth should override every other consideration; and perhaps he was right. For the second time that day I had to reappraise my conduct. I had the uneasy feeling that I had failed as a father as well as a husband.

'What happened after that?' I asked.

'After what?'

'After you left your mother that Saturday.'

He looked at me listlessly. 'The police keep asking me about that afternoon. I can't remember clearly. I got a bus into town and mooned around trying to decide whether to go down to Garston or not. I knew already that Anne and I could never marry after what I'd heard about you and—' He didn't finish the sentence.

In the end he had taken the usual train to Minford. He didn't remember it stopping at Clovering Halt. But he was in such a state that night that it might have stopped every half mile for all he would have noticed.

'You didn't tell Anne what your mother had said?'

'No, I put if off. I needed more time to think it out.'

Chris was positive about having seen Julia on her bicycle as Anne drove him to Garston from the station. He noted it particularly because she had been very much in his thoughts at the time. So when Julia stated, after her husband disappeared, that she hadn't been out all day, Chris knew she was lying and wondered why. That was the reason for his enquiries in Aberlandry. On learning that Julia had appeared to know her husband was dead even before his body was identified, he was sufficiently suspicious to get in touch with Lionel Wallis's lawyers.

'You see,' he exclaimed, 'I like Anne's uncle. And if he says he didn't shoot his brother, I'm inclined to believe him.'

'But you're prepared to accept that Julia did?'

He hesitated. 'I think it's possible,' he said.

Chris had refused to tell the police where he had been on the afternoon of the murder in case they questioned his mother. He didn't want her story about Julia and me to come out.

Telling the truth wouldn't have helped him anyway, for he had left Croydon in plenty of time to get the earlier train to Minford. He couldn't prove he had sat in the station buffet for an hour or more.

I asked him about the evening he had spent with Geoffrey

a few days before that.

'That was a funny business,' said Chris. 'He rang me up at the hotel and invited me to dinner at his club. Told me not to let Anne know. During dinner he talked scandal about people in the theatre and television, most of whom I'd never heard of. But afterwards, when we had a room to ourselves, he let his hair down on the subject of his own family. It was very embarrassing. I'd have said he was drunk except that he'd had hardly anything at dinner. He described his wife as a common tart and Jane as a potential juvenile delinquent. Anne was the only decent one, he said, and he wanted to be sure she'd come to no harm. Supposing she were left without a penny, would I still marry her? It was a silly question, but he harped on about it. I had to reassure him over and over again.'

'What do you think he was getting at?'

'I wondered if perhaps he was going bankrupt. Only that wasn't the impression he gave. It was more as if he were going to ruin his family by some deliberate act of his own.'

I had got much the same impression from my own conversation with Geoffrey a day or two before he died.

'Did he mention Lionel at all?' I asked.

'He had a few choice words for him too. And he said he was going to fix him. I gathered, though, that that was a different issue altogether.'

Again it tallied. 'A side issue' was the phrase Geoffrey had used to me.

Chris glanced at his watch.

'Dad, do you mind if—' he began.

'Are you in a hurry?' I asked, slightly nettled.

'I should be working, but that doesn't matter. I thought I might pick up Anne at the library. She'll be going off at four o'clock.' There was an animation in his face that hadn't been there for weeks.

I drove him back to London. Before I left him, I tried

to speak of Helen again, hoping he might have relented a little. But the hardness came into his eyes and he stopped me: 'I don't want to listen Dad. I don't want ever to hear her name mentioned.'

CHAPTER 11

When I got back to Garston, Philip Brent told me that Stryker had called.

'He took away the carbon of the manuscript. I hope that's all tight,' said Brent anxiously.

'Well, he's the publisher. I suppose he has to see it.'

All the same I was sorry it had gone to Stryker in its present state. My first draft was almost completed. But it was rough and there was no continuity between the chapters, after all, it was not yet the end of September.

'He's coming down on Saturday to discuss it with you,' Brent told me.

Stryker wasn't to be the only guest on Saturday. On Friday morning Julia looked into the study, where I had already started my morning's dictation.

'Busy?' she said abstractedly, and went on in the same breath: 'I meant to speak to you at breakfast, but Philip and Jane were there . . . Anne phoned last night. She's bringing Chris down tomorrow.'

'Oh! yes?'

Julia frowned. 'It's so tiresome,' she said. 'I thought that nonsense was over and done with.'

'Well, I'm sorry, Julia, if it upsets you, but I don't see what I can do about it.'

She didn't answer. She went over and turned up the thermostat on the wall.

'You need more heat in this room. It's much colder today.'

I waited. I recognized the symptoms—the nervousness

and the fidgeting.

Then she came out with it.

'What did Superintendent Caswell say to you the other day?' she asked abruptly.

'He talked about Chris mostly. Apparently someone's been trying to implicate him in Geoffrey's murder.'

I was looking straight at her as I said this. She coloured slightly.

'That's Arthur's doing mainly,' she said. Then, shrugging it aside: 'Did Caswell say anything about me?'

She had the hide of a rhinoceros. I put it to her more directly.

'Julia, have you and Durrand been trying to pin the murder on Chris?'

She sighed in exasperation, as if I had introduced an irrelevance.

'Lionel shot Geoffrey,' she said. 'Everybody knows he did. It was sheer spite that made Chris get up in the witness box and contradict me. And the worry it's caused me! So when Arthur remembered he had seen Chris about six o'clock that day on a bicycle on the hill road from Minford, he thought we should give him a taste of his own medicine.'

'Oh! it was Arthur who saw him, was it? And what was Arthur doing there at that time?'

'Arthur wasn't there.' Her tone was irritable again. 'He saw him from the window of his house.'

'You mean he recognized him from across the valley? But that must be a mile at least.'

'He had his field glasses. He's sure it was Chris.'

Julia seemed to see nothing odd in what she was saying and wasn't even much interested. At once she came back to her own worry.

'Did Caswell—' she began.

'Your name was hardly mentioned. But as a matter of interest, Julia, what *were* you doing when Chris saw you?'

She frowned again. 'It's so silly. I was never anywhere near the cottage. I'd been down at Arthur's and I was simply cycling home. If I'd known there would be all this fuss, I'd have said so at the start.'

'Why didn't you?'

'Arthur and I have been friends a long time. All perfectly innocent, but Geoffrey might not have thought so. So we—well, we didn't advertise our meetings. That Saturday I wasn't away more than half an hour altogether. Since nobody saw me go or come, I pretended I'd been in my room all afternoon. Then when Geoffrey didn't turn up and the police started asking questions I didn't like to change my story.'

'Isn't it time you did change it? The police know you're lying. Why not tell them the truth? Arthur could corroborate it, presumably.'

Julia was fidgeting again, abstractedly rearranging roses in a bowl at the window.

'As a matter of fact,' she said hesitantly, 'Arthur wasn't in—or at least,' she quickly corrected herself, 'if he was, he didn't hear my ring. I could have wept at having cycled in that killing heat for nothing. And I specially wanted to see him too.'

'Why?'

She seemed suddenly to repent of her frankness and she reacted with her customary rudeness.

'That's hardly your business, Maurice. You're here to do Geoffrey's biography, not mine.'

I had been too inquisitive and perhaps I deserved the snub. All the same Julia's habit of blowing hot and cold, of playing the *grande dame* when it suited her, made me angry. Even her condescending reference to the biography was insulting.

The only way to hit back at Julia was to probe her own weak points.

'Do you remember saying, Julia,' I remarked, 'that you

knew nothing about Geoffrey's two years abroad?'

She nodded, still haughty but becoming wary.

'But that wasn't true. You do know something, don't you? Something happened then that you don't want me to find out. You even got Durrand to try to persuade me to drop it.'

'No,' she said, but without conviction.

'What was it, Julia? What did happen in Austria all these years ago that still frightens you so much?' When she didn't answer, I added: 'Had it something to do with what you and Geoffrey were quarrelling about the night Brent overheard you — you remember, when you threatened to kill him?'

Her sudden pallor told me I had struck oil.

However, her reply was not what I had expected.

'I've got two things to say to you, Maurice. First, I didn't shoot Geoffrey, though, God knows, I had cause enough. The other is this. Don't stick your neck out: you're running it into a noose.'

The interruption had unsettled me. I couldn't get going again with the book and presently abandoned it for the morning.

Julia's statement about Durrand and his field glasses had started a train of thought. I telephoned Superintendent Caswell at Scotland Yard.

'Round about the time Wallis was murdered,' I said, 'there were a couple of girls camping in the field beside the cottage. Did you know that?'

'Yes. But we don't know who they were. They've never come forward.'

'Have you tried to find them?'

'Of course. But we failed. Lionel Wallis's solicitors have tried too. They hoped the girls might have seen something that would bolster up their case. But no dice. Old man Pearce did get a few pointers, but not enough.

They've vanished.'

I got on to the solicitors' office next. The facts they had were meagre. The two girls had arrived in Gleeve on bicycles on the Monday evening and, ignoring a 'No Camping' sign, had pitched their lightweight tent alongside the river. Luckily for them the estate manager was away on business and they camped undisturbed for nearly a week, leaving on the Sunday morning. The girls were about twenty, one dark, the other a redhead. The dark girl, who had been in the village store once or twice, was described as being American, but that probably meant no more than that her accent was not that of Gleeve and its environs. No one had heard her companion speak. After Lionel's arrest notices appealing to the girls to come forward had been put in the newspapers, but without success.

I had been phoning from the extension in the study. As I put down the receiver I was startled to find Jane standing just beside me. She had a habit of creeping in like that.

'I didn't know we'd Perry Mason staying with us,' she remarked pertly.

'You shouldn't have been listening.'

'I wasn't listening, I was just waiting. You've been on that phone for half an hour solid.'

I smiled an apology. 'He came back last night, didn't he?'

She nodded. 'Yes, Tony's back, thank goodness. This place is paralysed when he's away.'

I followed her out into the hall, where she made a beeline for the main telephone. As she was dialling, I asked her whether there were field glasses in the house.

She looked at me with tolerant resignation.

'Field glasses? Better ask Mummy. Or Trotsky—he knows every stick in the house.'

I heard from the telephone a click and the crackle of an answering voice. Jane's face relaxed into dreamy contentment.

'Tony boy,' she was saying as I moved away, 'it's OK about tomorrow night. I asked her this morning. A pushover. So long as . . .' I had moved out of earshot.

Trotsky did know where the field glasses were and fetched them.

'I'm having a morning off,' I said to him. 'Care to come for a walk?'

Brent needed no persuasion. My rate of progress with the book had taxed his endurance, for as a typist he was painstaking rather than fast.

We went out the back way, past the apple trees down to the wicket gate.

'Where exactly did you sit that day, Philip?' I asked him.

'What day?'

'I'm sorry. I'm thinking about the day Geoffrey died. You spent the afternoon in a shady spot on the grass, you told me.'

'Oh! that . . . Yes, it was under one of these trees—that one, I think. Yes, I'm sure that was it.' He was pointing to the biggest of the apple trees.

'And that's where you were when you saw Julia arrive back on her bicycle?'

'Yes.'

I went over and stood under the tree. It wasn't more than thirty yards from the gate, and the track outside could be clearly seen. If Brent was here when Julia cycled up to the gate he was bound to recognize her.

From somewhere behind me there was the hum of a motor mower. I turned round. The sound grew louder as the machine, driven by the gardener, emerged into view at the side of the house. It canted dangerously as it went over the side of a small hillock, then righted itself on the level ground beyond. I recognized the hillock: it was where Jane had lain with her transistor radio that afternoon. It was outside the library window on the west gable of the house. But that meant . . .

'Philip,' I said, 'You didn't see anyone else that afternoon, did you?'

'No.'

'Or hear anything?'

'No. Should I have?'

'Jane was lying on the grass with a radio on.'

'Where?'

'Outside the library.'

'Well, that explains it. You can't see the library window from here. It's round the side of the house. You wouldn't hear much either.'

'She was far enough out to be visible. I can see the spot from here.'

Brent was becoming petulant. 'I was sleeping most of the time. But anyway what are you driving at? Are you suggesting I told a lie?'

I laughed. 'Sorry, Philip. This detective bug has really got me. I'll be suspecting myself next. Come on, let's go.'

All the same I wondered why I hadn't noticed Brent under the tree when I was out chatting to Jane.

Julia was right: it had turned much colder. A wind was getting up too, shaking loose from the trees the first of the autumn leaves.

We had joined the Cresswell Farm road and were about thirty yards short of the main road when I stopped.

'This is where Julia was when Chris saw her that night,' I remarked. 'She was cycling back the way we've just come.'

Brent nodded but didn't speak. He was still sulking.

The lane leading to the back of Durrand's house turned off to the right a few yards in front of where we stood. Julia's story was that she had come out of that lane and had just turned up the farm road towards Garston when

Chris spotted her.

It could be true. But she might equally have been on her way back from Lionel's cottage.

I put the field glasses to my eyes and gazed across the valley. The lower reaches of the hill on the other side were thickly wooded and it was only on the upper slopes that I could see the line of the track. Even with the glasses it looked very far away.

'I don't believe you could recognize anybody from this distance,' I said. 'On the lane on the other side, I mean.'

'Who says you could?'

'Arthur Durrand. He says he saw Chris cycling down there that night.'

Brent adjusted the glasses and trained them on the hillside.

'*He's* a liar, then,' he said tersely. Our common dislike of Durrand made him forget his sulks.

We walked to the road junction, crossed the main road, and continued down the track to Lionel Wallis's cottage. The garden, I noticed, was rank with weeds.

I tried to visualize a third person arriving at the cottage that night, after Geoffrey was already inside with his brother. How had he come, this Mr X, as Superintendent Caswell referred to him? By car? By bicycle? On foot?

These campers might have seen him arrive. If only they could be traced . . .

A dog appeared through a gap in the hedge, a big black mongrel, with an ugly, friendly face. It had an empty peach tin in its mouth, which it dropped at our feet, wagging a tentative tail. Brent picked up the tin and flung it over the hedge. The dog bounded off in pursuit and was back within seconds, its tail now erect.

We were standing in the lane outside the cottage, just about where Geoffrey's car had been parked. The hawthorn hedge was high on both sides here.

'These girls wouldn't see much here,' I remarked. 'The

whole cottage would be hidden.'

'What?' said Brent absently. He was playing with the dog.

'The campers. I was wondering whether they could have seen anything.'

'Oh! yes. Where was their tent, anyway?'

'Over there.' I pointed through the hedge.

We walked down to a gap in the hedge a few yards further on and turned into the field, the dog followed us happily.

I remembered where I had seen the tent, some fifty yards to the left and quite near the river. And indeed when I got there I saw a charred bit of grass where there had been a fire and holes that might have been made by tent pegs.

I looked at the ruined bridge and at the track rising beyond it on the other side; and at the ford, not twenty yards from where the girls' tent had been.

'Unless they were actually inside their tent,' I said, 'they'd be bound to see anybody crossing the ford.'

But Brent wasn't listening. He was still having fun with the dog. As I spoke, he threw the tin a little too far; it landed on the bank of the stream, teetered on the edge, then rolled in. After gazing reproachfully into the water, the dog philosophically trotted away. Almost at once he was back, with another tin in his mouth.

'He must have a cache,' said Brent.

'He has—look!' I had seen where the dog had picked up the tin. There were several others lying nearby.

When we went over we saw what had happened. The dog had rooted up a lot of empty tins and other rubbish that somebody had buried.

'Campers,' said Brent. 'There's too much for just a picnic.'

'Our two friends, I think. Campers aren't allowed here as a rule.'

It was the kind of debris you would expect—tins, mostly,

eggshells, a plastic bag filled with tea leaves, the shattered fragments of a cup.

Then I saw half a picture postcard jammed inside one of the tins. The picture was of a big waterfall—either Niagara or Victoria, by the look of it. Of the caption only the word 'Falls' remained. On the back was the usual sort of message: 'Visited here last weekend. Just as impressive as the picture. Missing you, though. Love, Al.' The ink was smudged but still legible. The address part of the card was missing.

We raked through the rubbish in search of the other half of the card. Brent's fastidious nose wrinkled in distaste as he fingered the messy tins, but he was as keen as I to find it. The dog watched expectantly for a while but, getting no encouragement, soon drifted off.

We found it at last, not in the cache itself but lying crumpled in the grass some yards away. It must have been blown there or perhaps been carried by the dog. This time the decomposition of the writing was more advanced, but it was still just possible to decipher it. The card was addressed to 'Miss Bridget R. Wannaker, St Anne's College, Oxford, England.' And on the face the word 'Victoria' completed the caption.

PART III

CHAPTER 1

Finding that postcard marked a turning point for me. Until then establishing the facts of Geoffrey Wallis's death had been important to me primarily as his biographer. Now the excitement of the chase itself gripped me.

When I got back to Garston, I telephoned a friend at Balliol and asked him to find out what he could about Miss Wannaker and her companion.

He rang back the same evening. Miss Wannaker was an American student from the University of Pennsylvania, who had spent the past academic year at Oxford under an exchange scholarship. After term ended she had gone on a short camping holiday with an English girl, also a student of St Anne's, before returning to the States. The other girl, whose name was Vera Murray, lived in Reading; and I was given her address.

When I phoned the Murrays, I learned that Vera was in Paris, attending a summer school at the Sorbonne. She had left Reading at the beginning of August and would be home in ten days' time.

Mrs Murray told me that Bridget Wannaker had sailed for New York the same day Vera left for Paris. She was sure that neither girl realized they had been so close to the cottage where Geoffrey Wallis was shot. The news of his death and of his brother's arrest had broken just before they left the country, but at that time the precise location of the cottage had not been stated and there had been no appeal for the campers to come forward.

When I telephoned Superintendent Caswell to tell him what I had discovered, he listened politely and made perfunctory noises of gratitude. But his mind was on something else.

'There have been developments here,' he said at length. 'That's all I can say on the phone. But I must warn you again to watch your step. Don't discuss the case with anyone. With *anyone*,' he repeated, more emphatically.

'Are you warning me against anyone in particular?' I asked.

Caswell hesitated. 'No,' he said. But his voice betrayed him.

'Another thing,' he added: 'Don't be so free with these phone calls to me. Someone might overhear. If you find out anything, come and see me.'

'All right,' I replied, sceptically.

He caught the derisory tone. 'Dr Slater,' he said stiffly, 'I'm trying to tell you that you may be in danger. You've been asking questions and you may have found out more than is healthy for you. Be careful, that's all I ask. Just reflect how the Wallis murder was planned. That's the kind of person we're up against. Anyway,' he added more amiably, 'thanks for the tip about the two girls. I'll get on to that right away.'

Two things stood out from that conversation with Caswell. The first was that he no longer believed Lionel guilty: that was implicit in all he had said. Secondly, his warning against using the telephone at Garston seemed to imply that the murderer was normally there. But at present the only people living at Garston besides myself were Julia and Philip Brent. And, of course, Jane.

Afterwards I wished I had mentioned to Caswell the invasion that was to descend upon Garston the next day. It wasn't planned—it couldn't have been planned—yet, when I realized we were going to have under one roof everyone, apart from Lionel, who might conceivably have been concerned in Geoffrey's death, I felt a chill of foreboding.

I wakened that Saturday morning to a rhythmic tapping noise: a branch of lilac, half snapped off, was
beating a tattoo on my bedroom window. The wind had
freshened during the night and dark clouds were piling
up ominously in the north-west. As I looked out, the first
scurry of rain spattered the window pane.

Although it wasn't yet eight o'clock when I went downstairs, Julia had already breakfasted and was smoking a
cigarette while she skimmed through the papers and
listened with half an ear to the wireless.

'. . . issues the following gale warning to all shipping
in . . .' She switched it off when she saw me come in.

'Good morning, Julia.'

She barely acknowledged my greeting. When she had
something on her mind, she had no time for the civilities.

'I've been thinking, Maurice,' she said. 'It's so
tiresome'(her favourite adjective, this) 'that Anne's bringing Chris down this afternoon. Couldn't you—no, I suppose you wouldn't.'

'Couldn't I what?'

'Well, I just wondered if you might take them out for
dinner somewhere. Arthur will be furious when he finds
Chris here.'

'Well, why not put Arthur off?'

'I've thought of that, but—no, I can't.'

She dropped the subject as Jane came in, wearing pyjamas and dressing gown, her hair swinging loosely.

'What a lousy day,' she remarked, with a glance at the
window.

She was in good spirits all the same.

'I phoned Anne last night,' she said to her mother 'She
says I can wear her green sheath tonight.'

'But that's ridiculous, darling—it's far too sophisticated for you.'

Julia was frowning, but hadn't lifted her eyes from the

newspaper. Poor Jane! Her mother never seemed to give undivided attention to her.

This morning, however, Jane was unabashed.

'Well,' she said cheerfully, 'you'll just have to lump it, Mummy, because that's what I'm wearing.'

Julia did look up now, still frowning but defeated. 'I can't think why Anne's letting you have it.'

'She'd have given me her whole wardrobe if I'd wanted it, she's so starry-eyed about getting Chris back. And I'm glad too,' she added truculently, glaring at Julia, 'and I hope you're not going to be beastly to him again.'

'Where are you going tonight, Jane?' I interposed hastily, trying to avert a scene.

'Tony's. It's his sister's twenty-first and there's to be a party at the house. Tony asked me. It goes on till one o'clock and I've to get permission for staying to the end.'

She stuffed a piece of toast into her mouth with a defiant glance at her mother, as if fearing that the permission might now be retracted. But Julia had returned to her paper.

Owen Stryker came bustling in just before lunch. I met him in the hall.

'By God, what a day!' he exclaimed, as he took his coat off. 'Listen to the wind. The old jalopy nearly took to the air once or twice.'

He thumped his dispatch case. 'It's here, Professor. I've read it. Alpha query minus, to use your own jargon. Damned good, in fact.'

I felt absurdly pleased, like a schoolboy whose essay has been praised.

'Mind you,' he added, 'one or two bits, here and there—but enough of that just now. Where's your liquor, Julia?'

And he refused to discuss the book till after lunch.

The 'one or two bits here and there' were enough to keep the discussion raging all afternoon. Many of his suggestions I accepted at once. He was quick to detect the loose or repetitive phrase, the weak argument, the failure in objectivity.

Where we disagreed sharply was over his policy excisions. He seemed to me hypersensitive to the threat of libel, and many references to Geoffrey's contemporaries were watered down or, occasionally, cut out altogether. Even the brief sketch I had given of Julia's character, in which I had leant over backwards to be fair to her, was further modified in her favour. It no longer surprised me that Geoffrey and Stryker had been at loggerheads over the publication of the diaries.

Although I fought a rearguard action all afternoon, Stryker, apart from a few token concessions, won all along the line. His final argument was decisive.

'What you're overlooking, Slater,' he said, 'is that I'm prepared to publish a biography of Geoffrey Wallis that isn't what the public expects or wants. This Wallis'—he tapped the manuscript—'isn't the man they knew on TV. I believe it's the true Wallis, but that's beside the point. It's controversial and I'm taking a risk in backing it. I'm damned if I'll add to the risk by letting you have a swipe at other people as well.'

I gave in then. At once the mask of geniality was back.

'Don't misunderstand me, Professor. You've done a first-class job. Thank the Lord we didn't give it to that old woman, Andrew Clynes. He'd have soaked it in whitewash.'

'There's one thing I ought to mention,' I said.

'Yes?'

'I've used the material you gave me about Geoffrey's spell abroad. But it doesn't amount to much, does it? I'm going across myself next week to see if I can find out any more.'

Stryker's eyes narrowed. 'You haven't much time, you know. You've got all this'--he pointed to the typescript—'to lick into shape. It's pretty rough at the edges yet, you admit yourself. And—'

'I still think it would be worthwhile.'

He gazed at me for a moment, then shrugged. 'OK, Professor, have it your own way. But you'll never find anything after twenty-five years. I doubt if there's anything to find.'

He stretched himself and looked at his watch.

'God! Look at the time,' he said. 'After six! The bees'll be buzzing already. We'd better join them.'

We both got up.

'I meant to ask you,' he remarked, as I opened the door, 'did those missing pages ever turn up? You know, the ones that were torn out from Geoffrey's diary?'

'No.'

'A pity,' he said. 'They might have been useful.'

When we went into the living-room a few minutes later, they were all there, all except Jane, who was upstairs dressing for her party.

Anne had stayed on in London till Chris came off duty and had then driven him down. She looked radiantly happy, quite transformed from the dejection of the past weeks. Chris too was exuding contentment. It gave me a momentary pang to think how casually, without a backward glance, he had snapped the bond that had linked him so closely to his mother. I must see Helen again, I decided. I must try to soften the blow.

Julia's fears of a clash between Chris and Arthur Durrand appeared to be groundless. There was Durrand, whisky glass in hand, launched on one of his legal anecdotes, with a bored Philip Brent for his audience. The glow on Durrand's face indicated that this wasn't his first drink of the evening.

Julia came over to speak to Stryker and me.

'Well?' she enquired, 'and how has my protégé acquitted himself?'

'Brilliantly,' said Stryker. 'He's wasting his talents in the academic backwaters.'

'I knew he could do it. Geoffrey always said Maurice was the ablest man he knew.'

'I'm not sure Geoffrey would have approved of this book, all the same. It's not a flattering portrait, is it?'

Julia shrugged indifferently. 'He's not here to quibble about it, is he? . . . By the way, Owen, you'll stay tonight, won't you? We can easily put you up.'

The invitation surprised me; evidently his political views were not after all being held against him.

But Stryker declined. 'I'll wait for dinner, though, if you'll have me,' he said.

Under the influence of alcohol faces relaxed, tongues were loosened, voices became shriller, laughter more frequent.

Nobody heard the door open. I was the first to see Jane framed in the doorway, waiting to savour the sensation her appearance would cause.

It was dramatic enough in all conscience. A shimmering green dress; long slim legs and high-heeled silver shoes; diamond earrings; a string of pearls round her neck; her long hair piled up on top of her head; Cleopatra eye makeup.

For a girl just turned sixteen it was ridiculous. And yet not entirely so. It's so easy for the old and the middle-aged to look with the censorious eyes of the past and to miss the essentials. Jane had two qualities—youth and grace—that transcended dress and makeup. The golden tan of her shoulders and arms, the slim, supple figure, the shining eyes—these carried it off for her. She was magnificent.

I had two seconds' advantage over the others, just long enough for me to foresee with sickening certainty the hurt that Jane was going to suffer.

'You look wonderful, Jane,' I said, trying to forestall it; but her mother's strident voice drowned mine.

'For Heaven's sake, child, have you gone mad?'

And Durrand put in: 'Is it to be a *fancy dress* party, Jane?' and he peered round to see if his sally was appreciated.

Jane was fingering her pearls, bewildered, a half-smile still on her face.

'What—' she began.

But Julia was getting into full throttle.

'You're like a woman of the streets. And who gave you permission to take my earrings? Go to your room and—'

'Mother!' Anne's sharp exclamation silenced Julia. She went over to her sister. 'Dr Slater's right, Jane. You look stunning. What about my jade earrings? Come and—'

Jane shook off her sister's arm. She was tearing off the earrings and she flung them at her mother, her face contorted with rage.

'You dare call me a woman of the streets! *You!*' she shrieked. She stopped until she had herself under control, then in a flat voice she said: 'I know things about you, Mummy, all written down in Daddy's diary.'

'What do you mean?' It was Durrand who spoke.

Jane turned slowly to him. 'And you too, Mr Durrand. You were in it as well.'

Her gaze travelled sullenly round the others. 'And some of the rest of you too. Some of you wouldn't like what I read. You wouldn't like it if I told that copper.'

The silence in the room was accentuated by the howling of the wind outside.

'What diary are you talking about, Jane?' somebody asked. But I think we all knew the answer.

'The pages that were torn out. I've read them.'

'Where did you find them?' asked Stryker.

'They were still—' she began, but her lip was quivering. She suddenly put her hands to her face and ran sobbing from the room.

Julia made to follow her, but a swift look from Anne quelled her. Anne herself slipped out and ran upstairs after her sister.

The taxi called for Jane half an hour later. Anne had

done a good job. When Jane came down, there was no sign of the tears or the tantrum and she even gave me a tremulous smile. Her face, too, had been redone with more moderation and artistry.

Julia came out to the hall and managed an unconvincing 'Enjoy yourself, Jane'; but Jane flounced haughtily past her to where Tony, self-conscious in white tie and tails, was waiting.

Owen Stryker gave her a friendly pat on the bottom as she passed.

'I hope you've got your key,' he said. 'Everybody will be in bed by the time you get back.'

Jane scowled at him. 'They're leaving the door unlocked for me,' she said shortly.

A gust of wind swept into the house as the front door opened then closed. The taxi doors slammed, the engine started up, and they were gone.

We had dinner soon afterwards. The scene had been too ugly and bitter to be ignored and Anne was not deterred by the presence of guests from having it out with her mother. I had never seen her so angry.

'You surpassed yourself tonight, Mother. You've ruined that poor child's evening.'

'I didn't want her to make an exhibition of herself,' said Julia defensively. 'She was a mess. Why didn't you help her to dress? You could have toned it down.'

'She didn't want me to. Can't you see, Mother, she wanted to give us all a surprise.'

'She certainly achieved that,' Durrand interposed self-righteously. 'I agree with your mother, Anne: children shouldn't dress up like tarts.'

Anne's contemptuous retort was forestalled by Stryker.

'Don't be such a wet, Arthur,' he said. Then changing the subject: 'What I'd like to know is how Jane got hold of these diaries and where they are now.'

'I asked her that when we were upstairs,' Anne replied.

'But she clammed up. Something she read is worrying her, though, she did say that. She also said she spoke to you about it, Dr Slater.'

'Me?' I was startled. When I remembered Jane's mysterious remarks about scraps of paper she had recovered from the dustbin.

Stryker looked at me with interest. 'What did she say, Professor?' he asked.

'Nothing,' I said. 'At least, nothing that I understood. We were interrupted before she got very far.'

'Well, anyway,' said Anne, 'I've told her now to phone the superintendent tomorrow and get it off her chest, whatever it is.'

Someone—Stryker, I think—suggested bridge after dinner. Chris, who didn't play the game, volunteered to help Anne wash up. That left five of us. Julia cut out, and Brent and I started off against Durrand and Stryker.

My partner, Philip Brent, played an imaginative, undergraduate game, always preferring the clever bid or exotic play to the orthodox. His occasional triumphs were swamped by his disasters. Durrand too would be a loser over any considerable period. He was bold and timid by turns—the unforgivable fault in a partner.

Durrand and Brent cancelled each other out. But the other part of the equation didn't balance, for Owen Stryker was above my class. I was astonished once again by the sheer brain-power of this untidy, rather coarse little man. When he had landed an improbable slam by means of a triple squeeze, I asked him where he played his bridge.

'At Lederer's. You've got to be on your toes there to keep in the black.'

He was not one who suffered his partner's imbecilities in silence. When Durrand muffed the play of a simple contract that would have given them the rubber, Stryker commented acidly as he gathered up the cards: 'I thought even a lawyer would be able to count up to thirteen.'

Durrand glowered but didn't answer.

'How's business, by the way?' Stryker continued, as he dealt the next hand. 'Have the bailiffs moved in yet, or is Julia still pumping in the dollars?' Still Durrand said nothing. I wondered if Julia, who was sitting with a magazine at the other end of the room, had caught the remark.

Anne and Chris came back just before the rubber ended. Although Brent and I won it, we were a few shillings down.

All this time the storm had been building up outside. Solidly made though it was, the house was protesting and groaning under the buffeting of the gale. And from time to time bursts of squally rain battered on the huge double-glazed window.

Anne had switched on television but could get nothing but blurred squiggles.

'Another rubber?' Stryker suggested. No one really wanted to play; but we were restless and it passed the time.

This time Anne partnered me against Stryker and Julia. Julia was competent, but was playing by ear tonight, her expression abstracted and remote.

It was Anne who surprised me. Technically not nearly so accomplished as Stryker, she nevertheless outgeneralled him from the start. She made a psychic bid on the very first hand, which cheated Stryker of a stone-cold game; and shortly afterwards, when he rashly assumed she was repeating the gambit, he pressed on, was doubled and lost 500. He never recovered after that.

Sex came into it, I think. Stryker had more than a passing interest in Anne, and the primitive desire to shine in front of her tempted him into indiscretions that only brought disaster.

I had a certain sympathy with him, for Anne was being deliberately provocative. Chris knew what she was up to; I saw the conspiratorial glance they exchanged. No doubt she had old scores to settle with the amorous Stryker.

I ended the rubber by making a spectacular minor suit game, doubled in rage by Stryker and redoubled by Anne.

Anne added up the score. 'Twenty-three, I make it,' she said sweetly to Stryker. Do you agree?'

'I'll take your word for it,' he replied sourly, getting his wallet out.

'Did you hear that?' said Julia suddenly.

'What?'

'I heard a car outside.'

We strained our ears, but there was nothing but the whistling of the wind and the groaning of timber.

Durrand, who was nearest the window, pulled back the curtain and looked out into the blackness.

'By God!' he exclaimed, 'there *is* a car. It's at the door.'

I looked at the clock. 9.55. Much too early for Jane to be back, very late for anyone else.

At that moment we heard above the storm a thunderous knocking. There was something theatrical and sinister in the sound. Julia took a grip of herself and went slowly out to the hall. Driven by some vague protective instinct, I followed her.

When she opened the door, I saw over her shoulder, against the porch light, the silhouette of a man's figure but I couldn't see the face. Julia could. She gave a stifled scream and recoiled sharply as if she were being attacked.

'Not a very warm welcome to the prodigal,' said the figure at the door mildly and walked into the hall.

It was Lionel Wallis.

CHAPTER 2

Julia's social instincts were strong. Mechanically she took Lionel's hat and coat and showed him into the living-room. We heard the taxi drive away.

Lionel stopped just inside the door, blinking to accustom his eyes to the light, taking in the tableau that faced him, the silent group held motionless in various attitudes of astonishment.

Philip Brent was the first to find his tongue.

'Have you escaped?' he asked.

'I was released this morning.'

'But why?' There was fear in Julia's voice.

Lionel ignored the question. 'Do you mind if I sit down?' he said.

He had lost weight in prison: his clothes — a nondescript brown suit — hung loosely on him. His eyes were feverish and his voice thick and tired. He flopped into a chair.

I signalled to Brent to get him a drink. Lionel accepted the glass of whisky, but didn't immediately drink. He held the glass up to the light and contemplated it in silence.

He had a sense of the theatre, and he knew he had his audience captive.

'Glad you remembered, Philip,' he remarked at length, still fondling the glass. 'I always take it neat. Somebody else forgot, though, didn't they, Julia?'

Julia frowned but didn't answer.

'Yes,' he continued, 'that was a blunder. Almost the only one. A clever plot, I'll give them that.'

'I don't know what you're talking about,' said Durrand irritably, 'and I haven't time to sit and listen. I'm going home.'

'I think you should stay, Arthur.' There was an edge to Lionel's tone that brooked no argument. Durrand made no further move to go.

Lionel went on to describe how the murder was now believed to have been committed — very much as Superintendent Caswell had outlined it to me a day or two before.

'So Geoffrey slipped a mickey in your drink and then somebody shot him while you were out for the count?' Stryker sounded sceptical.

'Exactly. And they've now discovered where Geoffrey

got the mickey, as you call it, Owen. Powerful stuff it was. I was out for seven hours.'

All this time he had been abstractedly turning the glass round and round in his hand. Now for the first time he put it to his lips and took a deep gulp. We watched, fascinated, half expecting to see him collapse at our feet. Instead the whisky brought faint colour to his cheeks.

'Why did you come here tonight?' Julia couldn't hold back the question any longer.

Lionel smiled. 'The answer's simple: to see you, Julia. I thought if I could talk to you, I'd know for certain whether you shot your husband.'

'Go on, Lionel,' said Julia quietly. The rest of us sat silent.

Lionel had by now drunk most of his whisky. He looked much revived.

'Whoever shot Geoffrey,' he said, 'was a public benefactor, if only he'd stopped there. But he tried to pin it on me, and that I can't forgive.'

It wasn't in appearance only that Lionel had altered. The obsequiousness had gone and there was a hardness and confidence about him that reminded me of his brother.

Julia continued to press him.

'Why me?' she said. 'If you didn't kill Geoffrey, it could have been almost anyone. Why pick on me?'

Lionel regarded her with interest. 'Not "almost anyone", Julia. We do know something about this chap. He was well clued in on Geoffrey's plans and he was also able to take the revolver from Geoffrey's desk. That rather reduces the field, wouldn't you say?'

'It would still leave everybody in this room,' Julia's glance flicked contemptuously over the rest of us.

Lionel nodded. 'I've considered them all, every one. Jane too, for that matter. Where is Jane, by the way?'

'She's at a party. She won't be back till after one. But

you haven't answered my question. Why me rather than the others? It was the same in court. That dreadful lawyer man was trying to pin it on me from the start.'

'Julia, for weeks I've thought of nothing else. I've put to the microscope all the evidence at the inquest and at Court and everything my lawyers have dug out. And I've eliminated everybody but you—or, rather you and one other. Take your guests tonight: you're quite right—they were high on my original list of possibles. But for one reason or another they're all in the clear.'

Still Julia persisted. 'I'd like to hear your reasons.'

'All right. First, Dr Slater—he's got a complete alibi: he was never away from Garston all that day. The same goes for Jane. And Anne—her alibi's just as good. She left Garston at 6.30 and met the 6.42 train at Minford. Not nearly enough time to stop at the cottage and do all she'd have to do. Next—'

'Just a minute,' Durrand interrupted. 'You've overlooked something. Anne was out again late that night, I understand, driving Chris back to the station. She could have gone to the cottage on her way home. Not that I'm suggesting she did,' he added hastily.

Lionel nodded gravely. 'Thank you, Arthur. As a matter of fact I *didn't* overlook that point. But it's out of the question. The murderer had to go to the cottage at a time when he was sure Geoffrey would still be there and I'd still be unconscious. He couldn't possibly leave it till nearly midnight.

'Then an attempt has been made to implicate Chris Slater. It's been suggested that he came down by an earlier train, pinched a bicycle, rode to the cottage and shot Geoffrey, then returned to the station before his usual train got in. I don't believe it. Whoever did this murder is far too clever to take risks like that. The chances of being recognized either on the train or at the station or going to the cottage and back would have been too great. It's interesting, all the same, to consider who's been spreading that story about Chris, and why—'

Lionel broke off as the lights, which had flickered once or twice in the past hour, now went out and left us in total darkness. Everyone began talking at once, about fuses and torches and candles. I guessed it wasn't a fuse but a general power failure and I slipped out and felt my way to the back of the house for confirmation. From the windows at the back there was a clear view of some of the houses on the high ground behind the village. As I expected, tonight they too were in darkness.

A pencil of light stabbed out behind me and there was a smothered gasp.

'Oh! it's you, Dr Slater.' The voice was Anne's. 'You startled me. I've been sent for candles. Chris says it isn't a fuse.'

'No, it's a power cut. Probably the storm.'

The torch swung round the kitchen walls—it was one of those gleaming, modern kitchens designed and built as a unit—and came to rest on the compartment below the sink. Anne slid open the door and, after rummaging inside, brought out a box of candles.

But she didn't return immediately to the living-room.

'I wish I knew what Uncle Lionel's up to,' she said. 'He's got it in for Mother, I'm sure. And she's had as much as she can take.'

'Your mother's tougher than you think, Anne.' I was recalling her resilience after the shock of seeing Lionel at the door.

But Anne was unconvinced.

'No, Mother's the weak one . . . It's not only that, though. If Uncle Lionel's out of prison, it means that somebody else . . . You know, I've got that awful feeling that something's going to happen. The same feeling I had the day Dad died. There's—'

'Have you found them, Anne?' Julia's voice from the

hall was sharp and peevish.

'Just coming, Mother.'

Although it was nearly eleven o'clock, no one had made a move to go. Lionel's story wasn't finished.

Somebody suggested tea, but as there was no means of heating the kettle, we had a round of drinks instead.

'Well, Lionel,' said Stryker when we had settled, 'you'd reduced the field to four. I see I'm still one of the runners. How did you eliminate me?'

There were eight candles in the room, guttering with our movements and casting grotesque shadows on the walls. Lionel's chair was in one of the shadowy patches, and in that half-light the likeness to Geoffrey was uncanny. We might have turned the clock back eight weeks.

His voice dispelled the illusion.

'The last four have no real alibi,' he said. 'You could have done it, Owen. You left the cottage at six o'clock. It would have been easy to skulk about till after Geoffrey arrived, then come back in. But I know this: if you *had* killed Geoffrey you wouldn't have framed me. You're the one friend I can depend on.

'Then there's you, Brent. I suppose you might have slipped down to the cottage without being missed. But frankly I don't believe you've got the brains to plan a crime like this or the nerve to carry it out.'

Brent contrived to look relieved and offended at the same time. He opened his mouth to speak, but already Lionel had dismissed him and moved on.

'That leaves two—Julia and Arthur. And one of them did it.'

'I'm not going to listen to this nonsense,' Durrand blustered. But he didn't move from his chair.

Lionel went on as if there had been no interruption.

'They both had a motive, which is something nobody else had that we know of. Julia wanted to marry Arthur and Arthur needed Julia's money. They both had opportunity—in fact, Julia was actually seen cycling away from the cottage—'

'That's a lie!' Julia exclaimed.

'—All right, from the *direction* of the cottage, just before seven o'clock. She lied about it to begin with. And now, if her second story's true, then Arthur's lying.'

'What do you mean?' growled Durrand.

'Didn't you know? Julia now says she called at your house and didn't get an answer. Yet your were "pottering around the garden" all the time from 6.15 onwards. How could you have missed her?'

Lionel seemed to be remarkably well informed. I even conceived the absurd notion that he had been primed by Superintendent Caswell and sent here to see what he could ferret out.

Suddenly the lights came back on. All eyes were on Durrand, who had turned angrily to Julia.

'You said—' he began accusingly, blinking in the bright light.

'Yes, I promised I'd never mention my visits to you. But everybody knows about us now, Arthur. I had to clear myself, I had to tell the truth.'

'Well, why didn't you?'

'Why didn't I what?'

'Tell the truth. You didn't call at my house that afternoon. I'd have been bound to see you.'

'Arthur!' Julia was gazing at him in open-mouthed amazement.

Lionel chuckled. 'There you are. When thieves fall out . . . One of them's lying. Take your pick.'

Durrand got to his feet with a show of affronted dignity.

'I've had enough. But let me point out one thing, Wallis. Your brother and I weren't on speaking terms for the last three months of his life. It's ridiculous to suggest he would confide in me about his plans to get your precious document back.'

'He spent two hours with you in your office on the Monday before he died. Also; as I was saying earlier, it's significant that you went to such lengths to try to implicate Chris Slater.'

Durrand was frightened then. I could see it in the perspiration on his brow, the anxious way he ran his tongue along his lips. With the instinct of the weak he lashed out blindly.

'At least I never threatened to kill him. If it's a question whose word to believe, remember she did.'

Without a backward glance at Julia he walked out. A moment later the front door slammed.

Anne looked anxiously at her mother, who was moving around with a set, white face, blowing out the candles.

'You should get to bed, Mother.'

'I'm all right,' she replied gruffly.

'I must go too,' said Lionel. He sounded content, as if he had achieved what he had come to do.

'Are you going to the cottage?' Anne said. 'It'll be horribly cold and damp after lying empty all this time.'

'I saw to things this afternoon,' Lionel replied.

'I'll run you home, then. I'm taking Chris in to the station.'

She cut short his thanks and turned back to Julia.

'Mother, are you sure—'

'I tell you I'm all right. Leave me alone.' Julia almost shouted it.

There was a general drift towards the door.

Stryker remarked: 'I should be pushing off too, but I think I'll take you up on that offer of a bed, Julia. The weather's getting worse, and I don't fancy driving back in it.'

Actually the storm seemed to me to have abated a little and in view of Julia's state it was a tactless request.

Anne looked at him in exasperation. Then she turned to Brent: 'You see to it, Phil. That studio-couch makes into a bed. You'll get sheets and blankets in the linen cupboard. He can have a pair of Dad's pyjamas.'

As soon as Anne had left with Chris and Lionel, Julia went up to her room. Brent sulkily went about the business of transmuting the living-room into a bedroom for Owen Stryker, declining my offer of help. Stryker himself sat back and watched with unconcealed amusement. For all his powerful build, Brent was clumsy and inept at domestic chores. His performance wasn't improved by being under the sardonic eye of Stryker.

When the task was finished, Stryker gravely thanked him. Brent threw him a malevolent glare and went out.

'You're rather hard on him, aren't you?' I remarked.

'These bearded pseudo-intellectuals bore me. Especially the foreign ones.'

'He's not so bad, really, once you get to know him.'

'I know, Professor—just a crazy mixed-up kid, I expect. I still don't like him. Too sleek and silent. Like a cat. Let's have a nightcap.' He went over to the whisky decanter.

'What do you think of tonight's performance?' he went on, as he poured the drinks.

'Now that Lionel's in the clear, the last chapter of the book is as far off being written as ever.'

'Maybe. But Lionel's doing his best to speed things up for you. He flushed a couple of likely birds tonight.'

'Yes. He seemed to aim at Julia and hit Durrand.'

But Stryker disagreed. 'I'm not so sure. I suspect it was Durrand he was after from the start. Damned clever the way he did it. He's a changed man—I'd no idea he had it in him.'

The banging of the front door told of Anne's return. She ran upstairs but was back almost at once. She knocked on the living-room door.

'I guessed you two would still be up,' she remarked as she came in; then, catching sight of the bed: 'Heavens, what a mess. Philip, I suppose?'

She ripped the bedclothes off and started from scratch with quick, deft fingers.

'How's your mother?' Stryker asked her.

'Asleep, I think. I knocked on her door just now, but she didn't answer. She'll have taken one of her pills.'

Stryker was still probing. 'That must have been a shock for her, Arthur turning on her like that.'

Anne looked up quickly.

'The best thing that could have happened,' she said. 'Durrand's a louse. He was only after her money. As soon as his own skin was in danger he dropped her like a hot potato. I'm glad she's found him out in time.'

'Do you think Durrand shot your father?'

'I don't like to speculate. All I know is, it certainly wasn't Mother. There,' she added, straightening up, 'that should be more comfortable for you. Now, I'm going up to bed. Good night.'

I finished my drink and went up to my room.

Afterwards I found it hard to separate the reality from the dreams. The persistent tapping on my window—that was real enough, and so irritating that at length I had to get up and open the window and twist the branch till it snapped off.

It wasn't long after I got back to bed that I heard Jane's return. The storm was well past its peak now and the sound of the car engine toiling up the drive in second could be clearly heard above the wind. I even caught the murmur of voices as Tony took a long farewell of Jane outside the front door.

A very long farewell. It seemed much later that I heard the car retreat down the drive. But that was the point at which fact merged with fantasy. For Arthur Durrand was at the wheel, and I was in the back seat with Julia beside me.

Durrand was driving with maniacal recklessness. We shuddered round bends on screaming tyres and flashed, unheeding, across major intersections.

'For God's sake, Arthur,' Julia shrieked, 'do you want to kill us all?'

He laughed. 'Yes,' he shouted gleefully. 'That's what I want to do. They'll never hang me now.'

Then there was this great lorry filling the road ahead of us. With a final scream of laughter Durrand pressed the accelerator hard down . . .

I was back in my room then, sitting up with that perspiring relief that waking from a nightmare brings. But the bedroom had changed. It was long and narrow, and the air was chill. There were two other beds in it, two figures in the beds, sheets pulled up over their faces. I tiptoed over to the nearest bed and gently drew back the sheet, trying not to disturb the sleeper. I stared into the dead face of Geoffrey Wallis.

I knew where I was now. I was in the mortuary at Aberlandry. I tried to go over to the second corpse, but my legs wouldn't obey: I couldn't move. As I stood there, Superintendent Caswell came in with the morose attendant. Ignoring me, they crossed to the second slab and the Superintendent flicked down the sheet:

'Yes,' he said, 'it's Slater. He knew too much. I warned him not to open his mouth.'

The scene shifted again. I was in a tiny room, an attic of some sort. There was no light and it was hot and airless. Someone was panting by my side.

'We can't stay here, Maurice. We'll suffocate. Anyway, he'll find us.' The voice was Julia's.

As she spoke, there was a pounding on the door.

Julia gave a terrified scream: 'Don't let him in, Maurice.'

I found I was clutching something hard. A gun, by the feel of it.

'If you open that door, Arthur,' I shouted, 'I'll shoot.'

Julia wailed: 'But it's not Arthur!'

The pounding continued.

It was the voice that wakened me, Anne's voice, sharp and anxious: 'May I come in, Dr Slater?'

I fumbled for the bed light. As I switched it on, the door opened and Anne came in. She had a yellow dressing-gown over her pyjamas.

'I've been knocking,' she said. 'I couldn't get you to answer.'

I hadn't fully come to. But the anxiety in Anne's voice got through to me.

'What is it? What's wrong?' I asked.

'It's Jane. She's not in her room. Her bed's not been slept in.'

'What time is it?'

'Half past six.'

'She must have stayed overnight at the Parkes'. It was pretty wild last night.'

'I'm sure she wouldn't. She'd know we would be worried.'

Anne's alarm communicated itself to me now, because out of all my confused recollections of the night, one impression was firm — I had heard Jane arrive back with Tony.

'Does your mother know?' I asked as I got up and threw on a dressing gown.

'No. I thought I heard Mother calling. That's why I got up. But she's still asleep. When I saw Jane's door open and her bed not slept in I came straight here.'

In the eerie half-light of dawn we walked downstairs. We tried the front door. It was locked.

'She must have come in, then,' said Anne. 'I left the

door unlocked for her last night. She must be in the house
somewhere.'

Through the living-room door we could hear stertorous
snores.

'You don't think—' I began.

Anne looked at me levelly. 'She's not that kind of girl.'

It didn't take long to establish that Jane wasn't in the
house.

'Let's phone the Parkes'.' I suggested.

'No, Dr Slater, she's here somewhere, I'm sure. We
must find her.'

We were in the kitchen by the window. I looked out.
The aftermath of the storm was a light drizzle. The wind
had died altogether.

I was turning away when I saw it. Just within my line of
vision, on the concrete path outside the back door, a
shoe, a silver shoe. With a foot inside it.

She was half propped up against the wall of the house.
Her face was parchment white and her hair matted with
blood. I felt for her heart and was rewarded with the
faintest of tremors.

CHAPTER 3

Doctors, ambulances, police. So much bustle, so many
things to be done, that the full enormity of what had happened could be thrust to the back of the mind.

We let Julia sleep on. When she did waken, Anne had
already gone off with her sister in the ambulance and it
was left to me to break the news. Her eyes were dark-
ringed and dull and at first she seemed unable to com-
prehend. When she did, she became hysterical. The doctor who had examined Jane was still in the house and I
had to send him up to Julia.

By now the local police were on the scene, the same inspector from Minford whom I had met two months before, this time accompanied by a sergeant and a constable. They went through the motions, but it was a token performance; they were filling in till the CID arrived.

'Why does it always have to be a *Sunday*?' the inspector remarked irritably.

'What did the doctor say?' I asked him. The doctor — the police surgeon for the district — was a self-important, officious man who had snubbed me when I asked how Jane was.

The inspector shook his head. 'He didn't give much for her chances.'

At 8.45 Superintendent Caswell arrived with his squad of experts, and the local police, all except the inspector, gratefully departed. The photographing and measuring and the fingerprinting proceeded with routine efficiency.

And the questioning. But that wasn't perhaps so routine, for Caswell was in a blazing temper. As he came into the house, Owen Stryker, who had surprisingly appointed himself temporary cook, was emerging, shirt-sleeved, from the kitchen, bearing a tray with steaming cups.

Caswell stared at him. 'What the hell's *he* doing here?' he said angrily.

Stryker heard him and replied: 'Making coffee.'

The blood rushed to Caswell's face. But he restrained himself and followed the Minford inspector into Geoffrey's study. He slammed the door behind him.

The interrogations lasted all morning. Caswell saw each of us in turn: Julia, Stryker, Brent, a pale and frightened Tony Parkes, Anne, myself last of all.

Anne had got back from the hospital about midday, composed as ever, but very pale.

'They wouldn't let me see her,' she told me. 'They think her skull's fractured. And they talked about pneumonia.

She must have been lying in the rain for hours. Poor Jane . . .'

'She's not very strong either, is she?'

'What do you mean?' Anne's tone was sharp.

I had been reminded of Helen's remark that Jane had had a spell in a mental hospital.

'Well,' I said uncomfortably, 'I heard she'd had some kind of nervous breakdown.'

Anne was angry. 'That's the second time I've heard that story. There's no truth in it. Jane's never had anything worse than chickenpox. Who told you it?'

But just then one of Caswell's men looked in and said that the superintendent was ready to see Anne. As she walked out with her easy, graceful movements I wondered how much longer she could take the strain. If only her mother had more sense of responsibility . . .

It was after one o'clock before Caswell called for me. The air in the study was thick with tobacco smoke and, as I went in, Caswell was lighting a fresh cigarette from the stub of another. He was sitting at Geoffrey's desk, the uniformed inspector beside him, while over by the window another man sat with a notebook open on his knee and pencil poised. The books and other material I had been using for the biography had been neatly stacked on the floor in the corner.

The superintendent indicated a chair.

'You found her, didn't you, Dr Slater?' he began abruptly.

'Yes. How is she? Have you heard?'

He frowned. 'They're operating, but they doubt if she'll pull through. We've a man standing by.'

'What happened?'

'That's what we're here to find out.' He pointed to something on the desk. 'Do you recognize that? . . . Don't touch it,' he added sharply, as I put my hand out.

It was a heavy steel wrench.

'There's a heap of tools lying in a corner of the car-port,' I began. 'Is it—'

'That's right. That's where it came from. Anyone could have lifted it.'

'And this is what Jane was attacked with?'

'Well, we've still to get it analysed. But there's not much doubt. Look at the hairs sticking to it. And that's blood, that rusty mark.'

'Where did you find it?' I seemed to have taken over the role of questioner.

'On the grass not far from the back door. It had just been thrown down; there was no attempt to hide it. And no fingerprints, of course.'

Caswell sighed. He looked tired and dispirited.

'Well,' he said, 'we'd better hear your story, though I know it by heart already. "Fell asleep as soon as my head touched the pillow—didn't hear a thing." That's what they've all said so far.'

'I did hear Jane arrive back.'

'Uh-huh? Well, that's something. Go on.'

I told him what I had heard during the night.

'And you were asleep before the car went away?'

'I think so. I heard the murmur of voices—Tony and Jane, I suppose—then I think I heard a car drive off, but by that time it was all mixed up with a nightmare I was having.'

The superintendent was doodling on a sheet of paper.

'And that's all you can tell me?'

'I believe I know why Jane was attacked,' I said.

'Do you, now? That should be a great help.' I didn't detect the irony in his voice.

I described the scene the previous evening, when Jane announced that she had read the missing bits of Geoffrey's diaries.

Caswell's reaction was unexpected.

'Dr Slater,' he said, his voice charged with suppressed

anger, 'I've already had the same tale from Mrs Wallis, from your publishing friend, from young Brent and from the girl's sister. I thought *you* might have had more sense.'

'What do you mean?'

By way of answer, he asked a question of his own: 'What sort of girl do you think Jane is? How would you describe her?'

'You mean her appearance?'

'No, no, her character.'

'A typical teenager.' Then I gave it more thought. 'No, not entirely typical. A lonely child. Rather nice, but starved of affection.'

' "Starved of affection", that's getting near it. How does a child like that react to the indifference of her parents?'

'I wouldn't like to generalize, but I know how Jane reacted. She over-compensated so as to draw attention to herself—like wearing that extravagant getup last night.'

'Exactly. And wouldn't she be liable to romance a bit for the same reason?'

Dimly I saw what he was driving at.

'You mean, she may not have seen anything very vital in these diaries?'

'I mean more than that. I mean she never saw the diaries at all. I mean she's been murdered, or damn near murdered, for no purpose.'

Caswell's anger exploded to the surface now.

'Jane Wallis,' he went on, 'told me that same story about the diaries the day I was here last week. It didn't take me five minutes to see she was romancing. She wanted the limelight, that was all. Yet last night she had a roomful of people for her audience and not one of you, not one, saw through it. It makes me despair.'

'How are you so sure she was making it up?' I asked.

'I was suspicious as soon as she said she'd found the

pages in scraps in a dustbin. Whoever removed these pages from the diary would burn them, that's for sure. They wouldn't risk putting them in any dustbin. A couple of questions to Jane about what she'd read in the pages and she was flummoxed. She practically admitted to me she'd been romancing.'

'She didn't say last night where she'd found the pages—she just said she'd read them,' I protested.

Caswell sighed. 'If she *had* come out with that fairy tale about the dustbin, she'd have been safe. Our murdering friend would have known she was making it up. As it was, he must have assumed, I suppose, that she'd read the diary before the pages had been removed. All the same, you'd think he would at least have *tested* her story before he went the length of murdering her. Unless'—it came as an afterthought—'unless when Jane was talking about the diaries last night she accidentally hit on some fact that seemed to prove to him she must have read the missing pages. Tell me again exactly what was said.'

I reproduced for him the conversation as I remembered it.

Caswell sighed again. 'It doesn't make sense,' he said irritably. There was something deeper underlying his ill-humour, something he hadn't mentioned yet.

He asked me to continue my account of the previous evening. The flicker of his eyelids the first time I mentioned Lionel Wallis's name gave me the clue. But I continued stolidly to the end.

'Well, thank you,' he said briefly. 'I've no further questions for the moment. We'll get you to sign your statement later.'

I didn't get up. 'Why did you release Lionel Wallis?' I asked him bluntly.

It was touch and go whether I would get the snub I invited. But I had flicked him on the raw, and the need to justify himself was too strong. He sent his sergeant out on some errand or other.

'Between ourselves,' he said (the police inspector from Minford, who had sat silent throughout the interview, was ignored as if he were part of the furniture), 'between ourselves I had the devil's own job persuading my superiors to let Wallis go. And now the bloody fool has to get himself mixed up in this! You'd have thought this was the last place he'd make for the very day he got out.'

'You're quite sure he's innocent?' I persisted.

'I'm quite sure he didn't murder his brother,' Caswell replied, choosing his words carefully. 'If I hadn't been sure of that, he'd still be behind bars.'

While investigating Lionel's allegation that he had been drugged, Caswell had spoken to Geoffrey Wallis's doctor and had got striking confirmation of the story. Geoffrey had gone to the doctor a few days before his death and asked for technical advice for a crime novel he said he was writing. He wanted the name of a drug that would knock a person out for an hour or two without doing him any permanent harm. And it had to be soluble in whisky. The doctor had capsules in his surgery that satisfied the first condition, but he didn't know whether the powder they contained would dissolve in whisky. He was persuaded to give Geoffrey a couple to experiment with.

'Pretty irregular, surely?' I interrupted.

Caswell shrugged. 'Oh! I don't know. They weren't *deadly*, you know. Just powerful sleeping pills.'

The doctor's evidence had finally convinced Caswell that Lionel's story was true, and he exerted pressure until he got the charge against him dropped and Lionel himself released.

'And now this has to happen!' he added in exasperation. 'Just think what the press will make of it!'

'But surely it couldn't have been Lionel who attacked Jane?'

'I hope to God it wasn't. But there's no proof. It might have been anyone. Except your son—at least he's cleared now. He was back in London before it happened. We've established that.'

The telephone in the study rang. Caswell lifted it, listened for a minute or two, muttering monosyllables from time to time, then put it down.

'She's still alive,' he said. 'A fragment of bone was pressing on the brain, as far as I understand it. Operation successful, they say, but patient still very ill. The usual line. No hope of a statement at present. Not that she'll be able to tell us much anyway, I imagine.'

'What happened last night?' I asked. 'I mean, how was it done?'

Caswell looked at me speculatively. His anger seemed to be evaporating.

'Inquisitive, aren't you? Well, it's no secret. She was lured to the back door and bashed on the head with this not very blunt instrument.'

He explained. Tony had taken Jane home about 1.30 a.m. in his father's car. They had sat in the car till nearly two o'clock, when Jane got out and crossed to the front door. As he drove away she was actually turning the handle of the door.

'We believe she never got in that door,' said Caswell. 'It had been left unlocked for her. But before she got home someone had locked it.'

'It certainly was locked when Anne and I were down at half past six.'

'Yes. Very clever, really. What's the natural thing to do when you can't get in at the front door at two in the morning?'

'Go round and try the back door, I suppose.'

'Yes. You don't want to waken the household if it's not necessary. So Jane went round to the back of the house, where someone was waiting for her.'

'But if you're right about locking the door, it must be somebody who spent the night in Garston.'

'Not necessarily. Suppose for the sake of argument it was Lionel. He went home about half past eleven, didn't he? Well, he simply walks back up—it's only half a mile—some time after midnight, opens the front door and removes the key, locks the door from the outside and then goes round and waits for Jane at the back. Afterwards he walks back to his cottage. And of course Durrand could equally well have done it.'

'What about the key? I don't remember seeing it in the lock this morning.'

He pointed to the desk in front of him.

'There's the key,' he said. 'It was found on the lawn as well. Again no fingerprints.'

Caswell glanced at his watch. 'Good God, nearly two o'clock!' he said.

I took the hint and got up. But Caswell wasn't finished with me.

'The last time I spoke to you,' he said, 'I advised you to keep your mouth shut for your own safety. That's still good advice. The man we're dealing with is getting reckless. He's not entirely sane, I'd say; last night demonstrated that. And we're working against time. He may strike again.'

Caswell hesitated. 'What I'm trying to say is, if you're wise, you'll take my advice . . . But I don't suppose you will. That's why I've been so frank with you today. I want you to realize that if you keep on talking and asking questions, you may provoke a reaction, just as Jane did last night. And I want you to be better prepared for it.'

'You're not afraid of a second attack on Jane, supposing she recovers?'

'I've made it plain to the—to all of you this morning that Jane knows nothing. There's no reason now for a second attack.'

'You suspect someone, don't you?'

This time he gave an honest answer. 'Yes,' he said, 'I do. But it's just a hunch. No real evidence to support it. And no motive that I can see. It would do more harm than good if I gave you a name.

'By the way,' he added, as I opened the door to go out, 'I saw your friend in Paris.'

'My friend in Paris?'

'Yes, Vera Murray—you know, the camper. I flew over yesterday. Got back late last night. That's why I'm so tuckered today. A waste of time too. She'd nothing of interest to tell, except in a negative way. She's pretty sure no cyclist crossed the ford that evening. So that confirms your son's statement, but of course he's cleared now anyway. Oh! and one other thing. She remembers seeing Geoffrey Wallis's car arrive at the cottage that night. About a quarter past six.'

CHAPTER 4

I left Garston that same evening. With her mother in bed and her sister in hospital, Anne had problems enough without a guest to look after as well.

I was glad to go. I hoped I might see things in perspective if I could get away for a bit. Here I was too close to events and to the people emotionally involved in them.

Even the book had reached the stage where I could as easily work on it at home. But writing it had lost interest for me: the press of events made it seem an irrelevance. Only my Methodist conscience made me pack and take with me the manuscript and my notes.

I was passing through Gleeve when I was briefly drawn back into the web. Moving towards me on his old-fashioned upright bicycle was Arthur Durrand. He recognized my car and, with a rotatory movement of the right arm, he flagged me to a halt.

'I'd like to talk to you,' he said. 'Can you come up to my house?'

I hesitated.

'Just for a few minutes,' he pleaded.

I turned the car and went back the hundred yards or so to Durrand's house. I waited for him at the gate.

'Why do you use that bicycle so much?' I asked as he leant the machine against the railing. 'You've got a car, haven't you?'

For some reason the question disconcerted him. He peered at me suspiciously and said rather truculently: 'That's my car over there'—he indicated a light blue Hillman parked on the other side of the street—'but I'm trying to get my weight down. The doctor told me . . .'

The diagnosis was lost to me as he turned his back to put his key in the door.

Taking me into the room where he had entertained Julia and me some weeks before, Durrand offered me a drink and a cigarette.

He took a deep breath and said: 'There were a couple of CID men here this afternoon, Caswell and a sergeant. It was about Jane. It was the first I knew anything had happened to her.'

'Oh! yes?'

'Well, dammit, Maurice, you don't think I'd harm her. She's only a kid.'

I didn't answer. He was nervous. He had already downed a stiff gin and tonic and now he was pouring another.

'Does the superintendent—did someone tell him about—well, about that scene last night between Julia and me?'

'I'll be surprised if Julia kept quiet. You weren't very gallant, were you?'

'It's all very well,' he said defensively, 'but you don't understand what Julia's like when she's got her claws into you. She's a vampire.'

'She's the seducer and you're the poor innocent victim, is that it?'

'Well, I don't deny that to begin with I was interested. But she's so possessive . . .'

I took a shot in the dark.

'How much money have you had from her, Arthur?'

He flushed. 'That's an entirely separate matter. That's a business transaction, an investment in my firm.'

'A timely investment, though. You'd have been on the rocks otherwise, wouldn't you?'

For all his legal training Durrand in the witness box would have been God's gift to any competent QC. You only had to probe him and the reaction came like a nerve that had been touched.

'You were lying about being at home all that afternoon, weren't you — I mean, the day Geoffrey was shot?'

His hesitation was an admission. So I pressed on.

'And about seeing Chris — that was another lie, wasn't it?'

I ignored his blustering denials.

'But why—' I went on, then I guessed. 'You were on your bicycle yourself that afternoon. In case a cyclist had been seen near Lionel's cottage you got in first with this tale of having spotted Chris. That's it, isn't it?'

He gave a feeble grin. 'I knew it wouldn't stand up for long. But the police were breathing down Julia's neck and I had to create a diversion.'

'No, Arthur, it wasn't Julia's neck you were worried about, it was your own. You were down at that cottage. You shot Geoffrey. You—'

'No!' It was a frightened screech. 'You've got to believe me, Maurice. I never was in the cottage that day. When I saw Geoffrey's car—'

'You were there, then?'

'I'd been for a run on my bicycle, mainly to avoid Julia,

as a matter of fact. I was afraid she might call. On the
way back I thought I'd look in to see Lionel. I was going
to complain about the state of the garden. But when I got
down there and saw Geoffrey's Daimler parked outside I
cleared off.'

'What time was this?'

'Just after seven o'clock.'

Durrand was shaking now with fear. His character was
as flabby as his physique.

'Why did you ask me here just now?' I said.

'I'm nearly round the bend with worry. I had to talk to
somebody. I thought you might know whether the police
suspect me.'

'If they don't, they soon will when I tell them what
you've just told me.'

That evoked a new wail. 'Oh! Maurice, you wouldn't! If
they heard I was down at the cottage, they'd never believe
I didn't go in.'

'If you imagine I'll keep quiet about this, you must be
mad. I'd advise you to get your story in first. It would
come better from you.'

I felt no pity for him, even if he was innocent of Geoffrey's murder. He had had no compunction about lying so
as to shift suspicion on to first Chris, then Julia.

'By the way,' I added, 'Lionel said last night that Geoffrey spent a couple of hours in your office shortly before
his death. What was it about?'

Durrand was cowed. 'He wanted to change his will,' he
muttered.

'In what way?'

But at last I encountered resistance: he wouldn't
answer.

Mrs Beddowes greeted me without fuss and made no com-
plaint about the short notice of my return. Buxom and
even-tempered, an ageless fifty-five, she was the perfect

housekeeper, efficient without making a fetish of it, and friendly without being familiar.

She chatted to me as she set the table for a meal. Seeing that I wasn't anxious to talk about Garston, she quickly shifted to the current local scandal and to news of the University, on which she was surprisingly well informed.

It wasn't till I had finished eating and she came back to clear away that she mentioned the phone call from Helen. I had never spoken of my ex-wife to Mrs Beddowes, although I'm sure she knew about the divorce.

Helen had phoned an hour before I arrived and had left a message asking me to call back. But now when I rang there was no reply.

It was so unusual for Helen to contact me that I was slightly uneasy, but if it was important, I told myself, she would ring again.

Meanwhile I was slipping back into the old groove. Many of my colleagues were still away: those who remained were happily engrossed in an unedifying wrangle, which had reached the stage of lawyers' letters, between the Professor of Biophysics and the Registrar of the University. Beside that sensation, the murder of Geoffrey Wallis was of small interest, worthy of an idle question over coffee. I felt I was truly home.

Before many days had passed I was restless. I had started to revise my lecture notes for a course I was to give next term. But I couldn't concentrate: my mind kept returning to Garston.

I phoned the hospital twice a day to ask for Jane. 'Holding her own' was the stock phrase I was given. After two days of this I rang up Anne to see if she had any more news. She was guardedly optimistic. The doctors had reported a slight, but significant, improvement; there was now a real chance that Jane might recover.

The attack on Jane had affected me more deeply than the murder of her father. I could conceive of a sane motive for killing Geoffey Wallis, however much I might deplore it, but the attempt on Jane's life could only be contemplated with revulsion; all the more so since the person who did it had to be someone I knew.

I laid aside my lecture notes and unpacked the typed draft of the biography. I read it through from the beginning, resisting the temptation to amend and delete and smooth off rough edges: that could come later—for the present I was only searching for some clue to the murder of Geoffrey and the attempted murder of his daughter. I didn't find it; but one thing that did stand out was the inadequacy of the few paragraphs about Geoffrey's spell abroad before the war. Based on the scanty and unverified information Owen Stryker had provided, they were lifeless and unconvincing.

The time had come when I must investigate for myself. I phoned Chris on the Tuesday evening and invited him to accompany me, but he couldn't get away.

'Why don't you ask Philip Brent?' he suggested. 'He's still hanging about Garston like a knotless thread, getting in Anne's way.'

After my experience with Brent in Scotland I was not enthusiastic. However, he had studied German at Cambridge, which would be a help. So I rang him up and invited him. He accepted at once. I asked him to make plane reservations to Innsbruck on the Thursday.

Meanwhile I had one task to do: I had to find the address in Austria at which Geoffrey had stayed twenty-five years ago. I knew how I would get it. Next morning I drove the 150 miles to Bresford after breakfast. My mother had got my wire and had lunch ready for me. As always recently, I was saddened by the signs of physical deterioration in her. But her mind was as alert as ever, and there was still on her face that expression of radiant contentment that is given only to those who believe unquestioningly in their religion.

Her life now revolved round the little Wesleyan church she had attended all her days. When my father died five or six years before, I had wanted her to come and stay with me. But she wouldn't move away from Bresford, where her roots were.

Her one remaining ambition was for me to get a Chair. Every now and again she would send me a cutting from the *Guardian* advertising a Chair of History somewhere or other, even as far afield as Ghana or Istanbul. For her son to have the title of Professor would have satisfied a harmless vanity in her.

Geoffrey had been the great disappointment of her life. She had lavished so much love on him and he gave so little in return. In the last twenty years he had never visited her. A Christmas card, an inscribed copy of each book as it came out — these were her only contacts.

All the same my mother still treasured the meagre mementoes she had of him. A box in a cupboard in the sitting-room contained them — school report cards, exercise books, an album of snapshots, the few letters he had sent her when he was at University, and the tell-tale pile of meaningless Christmas cards.

I asked my mother about the postcard he had sent from Austria. She was able to lay her hands on it at once, as I had known she would. The picture was a conventional snow-capped mountain scene, which could have been anywhere in the Tyrol but which, according to the caption, was the view from the village of Marlos. On the back Geoffrey had scribbled: 'Think I'll settle here for a spell and try a bit of writing. Love to all the family — G.'

The one thing Geoffrey had told me on his return was that he had spent more than a year in a village in the Tyrol writing *When The Moon Is Low*. If Marlos was the village, that at least would give me a starting point.

'There was a letter too, you know,' my mother now remarked. And she handed it to me.

It wasn't much more informative than the postcard—a few lines describing the place, the people and the weather, a remark about the progress of the novel, and then a request for money.

'You would let him have it, I suppose, Mother?' I said.

As usual, she was quick to defend Geoffrey.

'I sent him £25,' she replied, as if she had somehow failed Geoffrey. 'It was all I had. If your father had ever got to know . . . But he paid me back as soon as he could afford to. Geoff was always very particular about money matters.'

'What does the PS mean?' I asked her. It said: 'Hope you like the enclosed.'

She peered at it. 'Oh! do you know, I'd quite forgotten. There was a snap with it. I stuck it in the album.'

It was among the last of the photographs in the album. Geoffrey was standing on the balcony of a house, his hair blowing in the wind, a brilliant smile on his face.

It was, however, only one half of the photograph, which had been neatly bisected through the line of this right shoulder.

'Was there somebody else in the picture?' I asked.

'It was like that when I got it,' my mother replied. 'Geoff must have cut it himself.'

I went back to the letter for the address: 'Gasthaus Hoffmeyer, Marlos.'

CHAPTER 5

The toy train that puffed up the Ziller valley from Jenbach hardly achieved walking pace.

Philip Brent, who was nervous about flying and had scarcely spoken in the plane to Innsbruck, blossomed out now that we were safely on land.

He was happy to get away from Garston, he told me; he

wasn't welcome there any more.

'Mrs Wallis has been very good to you,' I pointed out, 'keeping you on all this time.'

'I suppose so,' he conceded grudgingly, reluctant to see any good in Julia. 'I expect she had her own reasons. If you ask me, she was frightened to tell me to leave.'

But it wasn't only Julia who had aroused his displeasure. He was offended also by Anne's offhand indifference.

'Don't you see, Philip,' I pointed out, 'they're worried about Jane. You must be a nuisance there at a time like this.'

Now I had wounded him too and he withdrew into a sulky silence.

I wondered what would become of Philip. He couldn't stay on for ever at Garston and he wouldn't find it easy to get another job. If he had been exceptionally gifted, his outré appearance and exotic accent and affectation might have got by, but as it was . . . I wondered again why Geoffrey had ever engaged him.

It was almost dark when we arrived in Marlos after a hair-raising climb up the mountain road from the railway terminus in a battered old taxi. The Gasthaus Hoffmeyer still survived, typical of its kind, a four-storeyed wooden house, with sloping roof and flowered balconies round three sides. In the fading light I thought I recognized the spot where the photograph of Geoffrey had been taken.

As the season was all but over, we had no difficulty in getting rooms. Soon we were sitting down to roast pork and ice-cold Austrian beer.

Apart from a honeymoon couple from Germany, who had already retired to their room, we were the only guests. So we learned from the proprietor's wife, Frau Kapler, who had served our meal and who now hovered in friendly conversation.

I hadn't lost the fluency in the language that I had

acquired in prison camp during the war. My German was colloquial rather than precise. But it served. Brent, on the other hand, who was supposed to be a linguist, found it hard to follow the local dialect at first.

The Kaplers had taken over the Gasthaus in 1948.

'Hoffmeyer's two sons were killed in the war,' Frau Kapler explained, 'and he had nobody to hand it on to.'

I told her I was looking for information about an Englishman who had stayed here in 1937-38.

She shook her head. 'We only came to Marlos after the war,' she said. 'The Hoffmeyers are both dead. But—'

'What about records? Do you keep a register of guests?'

She trilled with laughter. 'For twenty five years? This isn't a hotel in the big city, you know. No, but if your friend was in Marlos for a year there must still be people in the village who remember him. Go into the parlour and see my husband when you've finished eating. He'll know what to do.'

The husband, a tall, grizzled, slow-spoken man, was taking his ease in shirt-sleeves and socks, a Meerschaum pipe in his mouth, his boots beside his chair. He listened to our problem and pondered it with the solemnity it deserved.

But his son, a handsome youth in a black leather jerkin, who had been strumming on a zither, apparently paying no attention, forestalled him.

'Frau Hans,' he said.

The father was a little put out but made the best of it. 'Ah! he's a clever lad, is our Franz. He's in the Forestry, you know . . . He's right. Frau Hans, who keeps the post office, is a daughter of old Hoffmeyer. She would remember your friend if he stayed here. You must see her tomorrow.'

The solution found, the subject was dismissed. 'And now, if you gentlemen would care to join me in a glass of Schnapps . . .'

★

I awoke to the sound of gurgling water. I put on a dressing-gown and went out on the balcony. The sun was already burnishing the sky in the east. Just beyond the road beneath my window was the swift, bubbling mountain stream whose murmurings I had heard. The pine-scented air was clear and sweet.

A child dressed in leather shorts and long woollen stockings was standing a little way up the road, holding a lunch pail and school satchel. Catching sight of me, he smiled gravely and called 'Grüss Gott!' Presently a bus came down the road and he climbed on. I looked at my watch: it was 6.30.

I found it hard to tear myself away, so peaceful was the scene. No wonder Geoffrey had settled here.

We set off, Philip and I, immediately after breakfast. We had nearly half a mile to walk to the post office, one of a cluster of buildings at the highest point of the long and straggling village.

Our progress was slowed by a procession of cows, their horns garlanded with flowers, bells round their necks, on their way down to the valley from their summer pastures on the mountain slopes: the first snows would soon be here.

Today, however, snow seemed an improbable prospect. Already it was hot enough for Philip to be mopping his brow and complaining of exhaustion.

After the white glare of the road it seemed dark inside the post office. It was a general store as well as a post office, one of only two shops in the village.

A woman had just completed the purchase of groceries and was leisuredly transferring them from the counter to her basket while she chatted about her family. As she turned to go, she caught sight of Philip and me, politely wished us good morning, and called over her shoulder: 'Here are your visitors from England, Rosa.'

Now that my eyes were accustomed to the light, I saw

that Rosa, the post mistress, was fat, grotesquely fat, her features puffed out and distorted, and her body vast and shapeless, like a feather-bed.

'You were expecting us?' I asked.

She nodded. 'News travels fast here.'

Her voice was hoarse, hardly more than a whisper.

She pressed a bell on the counter and a girl appeared from the back, a fair-haired, golden-skinned girl of seventeen or so.

'This is my daughter Freya,' Frau Hans briefly introduced her; and then, to the girl: 'Look after the shop, child. I must talk to these gentlemen.'

She heaved herself to her feet and waddled slowly with the aid of two sticks to the door through which Freya had entered, motioning us to follow.

The room she took us into was sparsely furnished: one leather armchair, a number of upright wooden chairs, a table and a bed, with a wooden cross on the wall above it.

She apologized for the bed.

'I can't climb the stairs,' she explained. My heart . . .'

She had eased herself into the armchair and lay back, panting from the exertion.

When she had recovered, she said: 'I knew your friend, Geoffrey Wallis. Why do you come here to ask about him?'

I explained that Geoffrey was dead and that I was writing his biography.

'I read of his death. He was shot, wasn't he? Are you from the police?'

I shook my head.

After a moment she continued: 'I nursed him, you know. For six weeks he lay in bed and I looked after him. Ah! he needed me then. *She* knew nothing about it.'

Piece by piece the story came out. I had to let Frau Hans tell it in her own jerky, repetitive fashion.

In the spring of 1937 Geoffrey and another Englishman

arrived at the Gasthaus Hoffmeyer for a few days' holi-day. On their second morning they set off with borrowed skis, but by lunch time Geoffrey's companion was back with news of an accident. Rosa's two brothers were among the party that went out and brought Geoffrey in. His right leg was fractured and he developed pleurisy from his hours of exposure. As it was too dangerous to move him to hospital, he had to be nursed at the Gasthaus. Rosa Hoff-meyer, the daughter of the house, then eighteen, volunteered for the job.

'I fell in love with him,' she said simply, 'and I think he loved me a little too.'

Philip sniggered and Frau Hans flushed.

'I didn't always look like this,' she said with dignity. 'Look in that drawer. No, the drawer of the table. Do you see the long green envelope? Bring it to me.'

Philip, shamefaced, brought her the envelope. She pulled out a photograph and thrust it towards us, saying: 'See, I wasn't ugly then, was I?'

It was the same photograph that had been in my mother's album in Bresford, only this one was complete. Beside Geoffrey on the balcony, nestled in his encircling arm, was a laughing girl, fair hair braided round her head, the very image of Freya, the daughter we had seen a few minutes before.

'Yes,' Frau Hans repeated, 'I wasn't so ugly then.'

Rosa's idyll didn't last long. Geoffrey had started writing while he was still confined to bed. As soon as he was able to get about he returned to Paris to collect his 'few bits and pieces' as he described it.

Rosa doubted if he would come back. But he did, two weeks later. And one of his bits and pieces was his wife. She was Italian, an art student in Paris, quite young — about the same age as Rosa herself. Pretty, Rosa conceded, but the fragile, clinging type. Rosa was not, however, an unprejudiced witness, for she had hated the girl from the moment she set eyes on her.

'Were they really married?' I asked.

'No, not then. But Gina knew her way around. She hooked him in the end, though much good it did her . . .'

Gina became pregnant and insisted on marriage for the sake of her child. And Geoffrey consented. They were married in March 1938. A few months later Geoffrey returned to England.

'And Gina?' I asked.

There was something like triumph in Rosa's expression.

'She died in childbirth in Taranto a few weeks after Geoffrey left her. And the child was still-born.'

'Well,' said Philip, standing up, 'that seems to be that.'

I looked at him sharply: there was a greenish tinge about his face.

'Are you all right, Philip?' I asked.

'I've got a headache, that's all. It's the heat.'

'Freya will give you something for your head,' said Rosa. 'Go and ask her.'

Philip went out quickly.

As soon as he was gone, Rosa said sharply: 'Who is that young man?'

'Philip Brent, Geoffrey's Secretary. He's helping me with the book.'

'I could have sworn . . .' her croaking voice began, but she didn't finish the sentence.

'Frau Hans, who else can I talk to here? Who else knew Geoffrey?'

'You don't trust me, eh? Well, if my husband had been alive, he would have told you plenty. Poor Ernst! He hated Geoffrey. Ernst was courting me then and he was jealous . . . But I'll tell you who you should see: Father Kammerländer. He married them in that little church across the road. He knew them well, especially Gina. It was Father Kammerländer who told me of Gina's death.'

'Is he still in Marlos?'

'He's old now and very frail. He had to give up the parish two or three years ago. But he lives not far away, in Mayrhofen, with his sister.'

She gave me the address.

As I was leaving her I asked: 'That Englishman who was with Geoffrey when he came here first — what was his name, do you remember?'

'I doubt if I ever knew it. He was only here for a few days, you know. He tried to get fresh with me and I had to slap his face. That's all I remember about him.'

Philip Brent didn't go with me to Mayrhofen. He announced he was feeling sick and would spend the afternoon in bed.

I made a rapid and alarming descent to the valley in the second of the three daily buses out of Marlos; then by train to Mayrhofen.

Father Kammerländer was in his garden. Despite the heat of the afternoon sun he was wearing a long black overcoat and thick woollen gloves.

'His blood's thin,' his sister explained. 'He can't get warm. The first snow will carry him off. He won't see another summer.'

All this in a matter-of-fact tone as she plumped a cushion for me on the garden seat beside the old man.

'He's very deaf,' she added. 'You'll have to shout. I'll leave you with him now.'

And she trotted into the house, a little, plump apple-cheeked woman who might have been any age between fifty-five and seventy.

The old man had been regarding me with a gentle smile, benevolent but withdrawn. His face was the face of a dying man, the eyes deeply sunken, the parchment skin drawn tightly over the bones.

'You are the Englishman, the friend of Geoffrey Wallis?' he said.

He smiled at my look of surprise. 'We do have telephones in Austria, you know. Rosa spoke to my sister after you saw her this morning.'

But I had been startled less by what he said than by the firmness and resonance of his voice. He wasn't so old as I had thought at first.

'What do you want to know about Wallis?' he asked.

'Anything you can tell me about him — anything that might explain why he was murdered.'

I shouted the words into his ear.

'Not so loud, not so loud, if you please!' he said, nodding his comprehension. 'I'm not so deaf as Maria thinks. She's a good woman, Maria, but her tongue wags too much. It is convenient not to hear sometimes . . .

'Wallis? He had great talent — genius, perhaps — but he was evil; if not in the eyes of the law, in the eyes of God. He had no piety or love or compassion. He had no soul. I warned Gina . . .'

'What was Gina like?'

A nostalgic smile came into his face.

'Ah! Gina . . . You have read Wallis's novel *When The Moon Is Low?*'

I nodded.

'Alas! I am not an English scholar. I had to read it in translation. There is a girl, the heroine, Dolores, is it not? That is Gina.'

'You mean, he modelled Dolores on Gina?'

'Yes. He made her Spanish, but otherwise — the very soul of Gina.'

In the portrayal of the tragic Dolores there had been a depth of feeling and understanding that Geoffrey had never quite achieved again. Her character dominated the book and largely accounted for its success.

'If that's so,' I remarked, 'Geoffrey must have been in love with Gina. He could never have written of her like that unless he had loved her.'

Father Kammerländer shrugged. 'Love? Perhaps. He was infatuated, certainly. She was his inspiration for that book. He even married her rather than lose her while he was creating it. But once the book was finished, she had served her purpose and he lost interest. He deserted her a few weeks before the child was due. I don't call that love.'

'And she died bearing his child?'

The old man shivered and pulled his coat more closely round him. 'No,' he said quietly, 'she lived for eighteen years after that. And the child, I believe, is still alive.'

While the appalling significance of what he had just said sank in, I listened with one fraction of my mind to his story of what had happened.

Father Kammerländer had been fond of Gina, who was not at all the fragile, clinging vine that Rosa Hoffmeyer had in her jealousy described. She had been deeply in love with Geoffrey and from the first had wanted to marry him. When she started his child she gave an ultimatum: either he must marry her or she would leave him and go back to her home in Italy. Geoffrey's need of her at that time was so great that he agreed to her terms.

'I knew what the outcome would be,' said the priest, 'but what could I do? There was no legal impediment to the union and I had to give it the blessing of my Church. Gina came to me again when her husband deserted her. She was heartbroken and would have liked to kill herself. I comforted her a little, I believe. And I gave her money to return to Taranto. I made her promise never to write to her husband or to try to see him. A few weeks later I wrote myself to Wallis in England to say that Gina was dead, and the baby too.'

'Why?' I asked him.

His tired eyes looked sadly at me.

'I am not a perfect man, Mr Slater. I make mistakes, sometimes I sin. That lie was sinful. I have asked God's forgiveness many times since. I did it to protect Gina.

Wallis was evil. He had done Gina harm enough already.'

'And Gina?'

'She had her baby—a boy.'

'She called him Philip, didn't she?'

He sighed. 'You have guessed? I wondered if he would be with you this afternoon. I would have liked to see Gina's son . . .'

'When did Geoffrey find out?'

The old man sighed again. 'It was Gina. She never stopped pining for her husband. And when he became famous, when his name was in the bookstalls in London and New York and Rome and even Taranto, she wrote to him. She sent him a photograph of the boy.'

'You mean she blackmailed him?'

'No, no, Gina was not like that. She just wanted him to share her pride in their son. And I believe he did. I suppose, like most men, he wanted a son. It is a daughter he has, by his English wife, isn't it?'

'Two daughters.'

'Yes, well, there you are. He persuaded Gina to send the boy to England to be educated. He paid for it, of course.'

'But he never let Philip know who he was?'

'He couldn't let anyone know that, not even Philip. It would have branded him as a bigamist. I hadn't known that he actually engaged the boy as his secretary. That was dangerous. Of course, my source of information dried up when Gina died five or six years ago. I miss her letters . . .'

He fell silent. A rustle of wind caught the pear trees and, as if in echo, the old man's frame began to shake.

'I must go inside now, Mr Slater. Would you be so kind—?'

I helped him to his feet. Leaning on my arm, he walked slowly across the grass to the door of the house, where his sister was waiting for him.

As he bade me goodbye, he said: 'She was a lovely girl, Gina. Wallis ruined her life. When you sit in judgement on the man who killed him, Mr Slater, put that in the scales.'

CHAPTER 6

When I got back to Marlos, Philip was gone. He had paid his bill and departed on the five o'clock bus, Frau Kapler told me.

'Ah! poor boy, he looked ill,' she said.

It was two hours before I could get a line to London. Superintendent Caswell was exasperatingly unconcerned about Brent's disappearance.

'Don't you worry about that, Dr Slater,' he kept saying. 'We'll look after that. Just you get the first plane home and tell us all about it.'

I was met at the airport next day and driven to Scotland Yard.

'No, we haven't found him yet,' the superintendent said in answer to my question, 'but it's only a matter of time.'

Caswell looked confident today.

'Tell me,' he said, after I had given him the full story of my travels, 'when do you think Brent discovered that Geoffrey Wallis was his father?'

'I've no idea, except that it must have been before Geoffrey's death.'

'Oh! you think he knew then, do you?'

'Of course. That was his motive, surely—revenge for what Geoffrey had done to his mother.'

There was a surprised silence. Then Caswell said:

'Brent didn't murder Wallis. At least we don't think so.'

'Then who did? And why has Brent run away?'

Caswell exchanged a glance with the detective-inspector at his side.

'I'm sorry, I can't say any more than that.'

He stood up. The interview was at an end.

'By the way,' he added conversationally, 'I've a message for you. Mrs Wallis wants you to ring her. You can phone from here if you like.'

A sergeant took me to an empty room and got the number for me.

'Oh! it's you at last, Maurice.' Julia's voice was peevish. 'How soon can you get down here?'

'What! Now? Today?'

'Yes, I must see you. We'll put you up tonight.'

It was so like Julia to take it for granted that I had no other plans.

'I'll need to find out about trains,' I began. 'I—'

She sighed. 'Haven't you got your car? Well, look, Owen Stryker's coming down this evening. Phone him and ask him to give you a lift.'

Stryker's green Vauxhall picked me up on the embankment an hour later.

'I hope you don't mind—' I began, as I got in.

He grinned. 'No. Glad of the company.'

'What takes you to Garston today?'

'I'm just looking in there for a moment to hear the news of Jane. Anne and Chris have been visiting her this afternoon. Actually it's Lionel's place I'm making for. He asked me down.'

Stryker's driving was erratic and alarming. Periods of cruising sedately with the flow of traffic alternated with frenzied bursts of activity when he wriggled through the traffic like an eel. In its way the performance was a *tour de force*, but the margin for error was too small for comfort.

During one of the quieter interludes I told him about my visit to Austria.

'Did you get proof of that marriage?' was Stryker's first question. 'Or that his first wife was alive when he married Julia?'

'Well, the priest said—'

'That's not enough. Without corroboration—marriage certificate, death certificate—we daren't use it.'

'Use it?'

He took his eyes off the road to glance at me in surprise. 'I take it we're discussing the biography? It'll give the sales a boost,' he added, when I didn't answer. 'But you'll need to verify your facts, Professor.'

His single-minded commercialism irritated me.

'Is that all you ever think about, Owen? Sales graphs and profit margins?'

'They're my bread and butter,' he said.

His eyes were now concentrated on a series of crablike sorties he was making on the road.

'However,' he went on, 'I'm not a fanatic. What did *you* want to talk about?'

'About what I discovered out there—whether it gives a clue to Geoffrey's murder.'

'Ah! that.' He relaxed again, having achieved an advance of three places in the echelon. 'Well, it does give some people a motive, doesn't it? Four at least. Five if you count Philip, though you say the police don't.'

'Four? Julia I can see. And Arthur Durrand. But the other two?'

He shrugged. 'The two girls. Anne and Jane. Same motive.'

'I hardly think—'

But Stryker interrupted. 'That's all you picked up in Marlos, is it? You're not keeping anything back?'

'No. Why should I?'

He didn't answer.

The traffic had thinnned out. And now that the opportunities were greater, Stryker had perversely lost his ambition. We jogged along at a comfortable forty-five.

We were passing through Gleeve before he spoke again.

'What did you say that woman's name was?'

'What woman?'

'The one Geoffrey married.'

'Gina. I never heard her second name.'

'Gina. Yes, it comes back now. She used to tag along with him in Paris. But I'd never have guessed they'd get married.'

'You knew Geoffrey when he was in Paris?' I asked in surprise.

'Yes. That's where I met him . . .'

They had kept dinner for us. Stryker half-heartedly protested that Lionel would be expecting him, but he was easily persuaded to stay.

Chris and Anne were there and, to my surprise, Arthur Durrand, clearly restored to favour with Julia and smug as ever.

The news of Jane was good. She was out of danger now and Anne and Chris had been allowed half an hour with her.

It was made plain to me that the subject of my visit to Austria was taboo. Clearly they knew what I had learned there and didn't want to talk about it.

Conversation at dinner was forced and spasmodic and soon languished. The vacuum was filled by a typically pretentious monologue from Arthur Durrand on trends in modern art.

As soon as he had finished coffee, Stryker departed. Durrand was still in spate, but Julia interrupted him without compunction: 'You'd better go too, Arthur. Maurice and I have things to discuss.'

Durrand frowned huffily, but he went meekly enough.

'And now, children—' Julia began.

'All right, Mother,' said Anne, smiling, 'you've made your point. Chris and I will keep out of your way.'

'So you know about Philip?' Julia began, as soon as we were alone.

'Did Caswell tell you?' I asked.

'He was here this morning,' she admitted. 'But anyway, as soon as I heard you were going to Austria, I knew you'd nose it out. You're so confoundedly thorough.' She made it sound a fault.

'How long have you known?' I asked her.

She shrugged. 'About Philip? Not long. Of course, I always wondered what Geoffrey saw in him. He was so in-efficient, and Geoffrey couldn't stand inefficiency as a rule. But I never dreamt he was his son. Not till that night when Geoffrey and I—' She broke off and laughed. 'Funny to think that Philip actually overheard us, and didn't realise it was him we were quarrelling about.'

She lit a cigarette.

'You don't like Arthur Durrand much, do you, Maurice?' she asked, going off at a tangent.

'I'm surprised you still—'

'Yes, I know. You're surprised I humbled my pride after the things he said last week. But I need him, Maurice. And he needs me too—and not only for my money.'

She said it defiantly, as if trying to convince herself.

'Arthur's got his faults,' she went on. 'He's a coward. Sometimes he can be a bore. But at least he's human. Geoffrey wasn't.'

I asked how long her affair with Durrand had been going on.

'Three years,' she said. 'Nearly four. It helped to make life tolerable. As far as Geoffrey was concerned I was a—a chattel, like his house or his car.'

'When did Geoffrey find out?'

She puffed nervously at her cigarette. She had an awkward way of holding it, as if she were unused to smoking.

'He'd never have guessed,' she said, 'If Lionel hadn't come here to live. It was easy to hoodwink Geoffrey. He was so conceited that it never crossed his mind I might be unfaithful. But Lionel told him.'

She confirmed what Ross, the Scottish lawyer, had told me—that Lionel's sole object in coming to Garston had been to make his brother suffer for the wrong he had done Lionel in the past. Julia's affair with Durrand was grist to his mill. He told Geoffrey, not from any grudge against her, but because it would wound his brother's vanity.

Julia went on:

'He was right. Geoffrey never got over the humiliation. For weeks he brooded until he'd lost all sense of proportion. Finally he decided to disown me—to shout from the housetops that I wasn't really his wife and Anne and Jane were illegitimate; and that Philip was his rightful son and heir. He gave me the whole works that night—the night I'm supposed to have threatened to kill him.'

'Supposed to?'

'All right,' she admitted, 'I expect I did say it. I was so furious . . .'

'That was the first you'd heard about his marriage to Gina?'

She hesitated. 'Well, no. He did tell me about Gina before we were married. But I believed—and I suppose he did too at that time—that she was dead. I never heard her name again until it turned up in the diary last February.'

'You read the diary?' I exclaimed in surprise.

She made a gesture of impatience. 'Of course. Any time I wanted to know what Geoffrey was up to, I had only to look at his diary. He didn't leave much out. A sign of megalomania, I always thought.'

'I thought he kept it locked in his desk?'

'If you imagine that after twenty years of marriage I didn't know how to get into Geoffrey's desk . . .' She let the sentence die.

Julia went on to tell me what she had read in the diaries. It was on 16th February that Geoffrey had learned about her affair with Durrand. The fact was duly recorded in the diary for that day, and the next day there appeared the first reference to Gina and to 'my son'.

'Of course,' Julia interjected, 'I never for a moment connected Philip with it. All I gathered (the wording was pretty cryptic) was that Gina had been alive at the time we were married and that the son was still alive.'

These entries by Geoffrey in his diary—perhaps four or five a month from the end of February onwards—had by early July crystallized in the form of a proposal to make public the fact of his earlier marriage.

'When I read that,' said Julia, 'I didn't really believe it. I thought his pride would stop him. But he convinced me that night we had the big row. I realized then he was mad: he was determined to punish me, no matter what the consequences were for himself or anyone else. And, of course, it was then that he told me about Philip. That really shocked me.'

'Had there been nothing about Philip in the diary?'

'Not up till that point. But the very next day he wrote it all down, the whole story about his precious son.' Julia's voice was bitter.

'And these pages in the diary about Gina and Philip and about the plans for destroying you—these are the pages that are missing?'

Julia shrugged. 'I suppose so.'

'What was the date of the last entry you read, Julia?'

'About a week before he died.'

'Was there anything in the diary about his plan for getting the confession back from Lionel?'

'No. He wrote at one point that he was going to deal with Lionel before he let the big news break. But there were no details of how he proposed to do it.'

'Incidentally,' I said, 'why *did* Lionel leave Garston? Did he really make a pass at you?'

'No,' she admitted grudgingly. 'I couldn't stand the way he used to spy on Arthur and me, even after Geoffrey knew about us. One day I rounded on him and told him he'd have to go. Much to my surprise he went without much fuss. I think he felt some remorse for what he'd done to me.'

Julia lit another cigarette. She still hadn't said why she had brought me here. She wasn't usually so circumspect.

'Have you told Superintendent Caswell what you read in the diaries?' I asked.

'I told him this morning.'

'You'd have saved a lot of trouble if you'd been frank at the beginning.'

'No doubt. But it's not agreeable to admit that your marriage was void and your children are illegitimate.'

'You discussed it with Arthur Durrand, though?'

The hand holding the cigarette paused in mid-air. Her eyes narrowed.

'Why do you say that?'

'Arthur tried to stop me from going to Austria. He must have known what I'd find.'

She sighed. 'Yes, Arthur knew. I told him. And anyway he heard about it from Geoffrey himself.'

'The day he called at Arthur's office?'

She nodded. 'It was a sophisticated form of torture Geoffrey had devised. He pretended he wanted Arthur's professional advice: what would his legal obligations be to Anne and Jane, supposing it were proved that he and I had never really been married?'

'And what did Arthur say?'

'What could he say? Geoffrey would have to contribute

to Jane's maintenance as long as she was at school, but he'd have no responsibility for me or for Anne.'

'Surely he didn't intend to cut off his daughters too? He was fond of them, wasn't he?'

Julia watched the smoke curl up from her cigarette. 'After his fashion I suppose he was. Especially of Anne. But he'd know that any money he gave Anne would be shared with me. So the break had to be complete.'

I was beginning to see what was worrying Julia.

'Arthur couldn't have been very happy about things,' I remarked. 'You were financing him, weren't you? He would feel the pinch if you suddenly became penniless.'

'I'd already given him all I could afford. I hadn't much of my own, you see.'

'Well, put it this way. If Geoffrey could be silenced before he blew the gaff, you'd be a rich woman. I take it Geoffrey's money *is* coming to you?'

She nodded.

'How much?'

'I don't know yet, but it'll be in six figures, they tell me.'

'And Arthur knew he was intending to disinherit you. He knew there wasn't much time . . .'

I was deliberately provoking her.

'Maurice,' she said anxiously, 'tell me honestly, do you think Arthur killed Geoffrey?'

'He could have. He was down at Lionel's cottage that night, at the time you called at his house. He admitted it to me.'

'Oh! God, I knew it! I knew he was hiding something. Do the police know?'

'Yes.'

She had got up from her chair and was distractedly pacing the room.

'You've no idea what it's like, Maurice, not being sure. Loving him and frightened of him at the same time;

wondering, every time you see his hand lifting a cup or lighting a cigarette, whether this was the hand that fired the gun at Geoffrey and smashed that spanner down on Jane's skull.'

CHAPTER 7

Sunday began quietly. Anne and her mother went to church while I lazed in the garden, enjoying the Indian summer. It was the first Sunday in October, but as warm as many a day in August.

The telephone rang and I went in to answer it. It was Superintendent Caswell.

'Oh! it's you, Dr Slater,' he said. 'What are you doing down there?' But without waiting for an answer he went on: 'Look, has Brent turned up at Garston?'

'No, he's not here.'

'He's in this country, we believe. He got back before the alarm was raised.'

Caswell's voice was anxious.

'Do you still believe—' I began.

He knew what I meant. 'Brent's not our man,' he said decisively, 'but we must find him all the same. Let me know at once if he turns up. I'll be at the Yard all day.'

After lunch Julia and I went to the hospital to see Jane. Anne didn't accompany us, because Owen Stryker had phoned and invited himself down for a further talk with her about her novel.

'Bring Chris back here, would you?' she said. 'I was to pick him up at the hospital.'

Julia drove her Morris Minor with a characteristic disregard for other road users.

'I enjoy driving now,' she remarked. 'It's funny how quickly you get into it. I'm sitting my test next week.'

She moved on to the crown of the road and nearly edged into the ditch a car that had been overtaking. The angry blare from his horn made no impression on her.

'I wonder if Philip's turned up yet,' she remarked suddenly.

I remembered Caswell's telephone call and told her what he had said.

'I can't understand why they're so sure he didn't do it,' she commented.

'He'd no motive. Unless you think he knew Geoffrey was his father?'

'No, he didn't know. I'd have seen it in his attitude to me. He could never have hidden that. I take it he's found out now, though?'

'Yes, he knows now. I think the shock was too much for him and that's why he's run away.'

I had wondered at first just how Philip did find out, for he hadn't been with me when I spoke with Father Kammerländer. But the answer wasn't difficult, Frau Hans, the postmistress, had told of Geoffrey's marriage. The name Gina, his mother's name, and the reference to Taranto, where he had lived as a child, would be enough.

'I wonder how much it'll take to buy Philip off,' said Julia.

'Buy him off?'

'Well, of course, the money comes to me by Geoffrey's will, and it doesn't matter a rap whether we were married or not. All the same, I'd rather all this didn't leak out. I'm prepared to pay for silence, within reason. That goes for you too, Maurice. I don't want any of this in your book. That's why I put your name to Owen Stryker in the first place. I knew that if you did find out you'd be discreet.'

I started to answer, but she wasn't listening. We had been climbing steadily for some minutes; now the road flattened out.

'I hate this bit,' said Julia, her lips set in a tight line.

'I've always been terrified by heights.' Our speed had
dropped to thirty, and she was hugging the middle of the
road.

For half a mile or more the road ran round the
shoulder of the hill ('Gideon's Crest', it was called, Julia
told me). On our left was a grass verge, unfenced and
perhaps two feet broad, then a steep drop—in places
almost sheer—to the valley a couple of hundred feet
below. The road was level and straight, not dangerous or
even alarming to the normal driver. But to one with no
head for heights, no doubt it was uncomfortable.

At the end of the stretch the road to the hospital branched
off to the right.

'Thank God,' said Julia, visibly relaxing as we turned
the corner. 'One of these days I'm going to be over the
bank.'

Jane had a room facing south with a view over the downs.
The sun was streaming in the open window.

'Not more than twenty minutes,' the nurse warned us.
'She's tired today.'

To me she seemed not so much tired as restless and
discontented. She was pale, certainly, and her head was
swathed in bandages, but she looked well enough.

'Did you bring my transistor?' she asked her mother at
once.

'No, Should I have?'

Jane was almost in tears. 'But I *told* Anne,' she said.
'This contraption'—she indicated the ear-phones above
the bed—'isn't working.'

'The cricket season's over now anyway, Jane,' I remarked.

'Even the news in Welsh would be a relief. It's so *boring*
to be cooped up here all day.'

I knew what was really upsetting her; Anne had told
me the previous day. Tony hadn't been to see her. His
parents had forbidden it, having decided, after a murder

and an attempted murder, that the Wallises weren't a suitable family for their son to get involved with.

Jane brightened when Chris arrived. Chris was very good with her; he could talk her language. And today he had a trophy which appealed to her more than all the fruit and chocolates and magazines that her mother had brought.

The current American teenage idol—a youth whose latest number had topped the hit parade on both sides of the Atlantic—was staying at Chris's hotel. Chris had persuaded him to scribble a brief message to Jane on the back of a photograph of himself.

'Oh! Chris!' she murmured, her eyes glistening. 'How did you do it? Did you actually *speak* to him?'

'As a matter of fact he was quite human. He wanted to know what had happened.'

'Oh! It was worth it,' said Jane, still holding the photograph with reverent fingers, 'it was worth getting bashed on the nut for this.'

I could see that already she was weaving a romance in her imagination. Julia saw it too.

'I wish you'd get this romantic nonsense out of your system,' she remarked caustically. 'That's your trouble, Jane. You have to dramatize everything. Soon you'll not know what's real and what isn't. Look at the way you had us all believing you'd read your father's diary. You'd almost convinced yourself, hadn't you? And see where it's landed you.'

I came to Jane's defence: 'That's not fair, Julia. To get nearly murdered is a pretty drastic penalty for a mild fib. And there was some excuse for it, after all. Jane was upset at being told off in front of all these people.'

'Upset? I nearly threw up,' said Jane, making a face at her mother. 'Imagine *you* calling *me* a tart. I *knew* there would be bits in the diary about you and the co-respondent, and—'

'Jane!' Julia was furious.

'All right—about you and Mr Durrand. So I pretended I'd read it. That old basket, Stryker, looked as if he didn't believe me. That's why I added the other bits—about Uncle Lionel and all that. How was I to know somebody was going to take me seriously at last?'

A nurse looked in. 'I think—' she began.

Chris and I said goodbye to Jane and came out first, leaving Julia, who looked somewhat chastened, to make her peace with Jane.

'I've seen Mother,' said Chris, as we stood outside in the sunshine.

'I'm glad.'

He waited for a moment, as if expecting me to say more. Then he continued: 'I know, Dad, that nearly everything Mother said about you was untrue, right from the beginning. I think I've known for a long time. Now I can admit it.'

I waited. I knew Chris: the sting was still to come, the sting in the tail.

'Have you ever asked yourself, Dad, what made her like that? Don't you think you may have been a little to blame too? You expected too much of her.'

I didn't answer. This time he took my silence for granted.

'I wish you'd go and see her just occasionally,' he added diffidently. 'She'd like that.'

Julia came down the steps towards us, apparently unruffled by her scene with Jane.

The moment of intimacy had passed. As I turned to open the door of the car Chris said lightly:

'By the way, Mother asked me to give you a message. "Tell him it was the wrong one," she said; "he'll know what I mean".'

But I didn't.

★

Chris's lips tightened when he saw Stryker's car parked outside the front door of Garston.

'He's still here, is he?' he muttered. 'If he's been pestering Anne again—'

'He came down to talk about her novel,' I reminded him.

He gave a disbelieving grunt. 'I know. It's as good an excuse as any other . . .'

Anne came out of the living-room when she heard us arrive. Rolling her eyes expressively and indicating the room behind her, she remarked *sotto voce*: 'He's been up to his tricks again.'

'Wait till I get my hands on him,' said Chris angrily, striding towards the door.

Anne restrained him. 'Don't, Chris. He didn't get beyond the fatherly knee-patting stage. And it's cheap at the price, for he's agreed to publish.' She turned to me. 'Uncle Lionel was on the phone, Dr Slater. He'd like you to go down and see him.'

'Now?'

'Before 5.30 if possible. There's someone he wants you to meet.'

It was ten to five now. I declined Julia's offer of her car and walked down to the village in the sunshine.

Lionel was in his garden in his shirt-sleeves, wielding a hoe. There was no sign of the visitor I was to meet.

'My landlord's been complaining again about the weeds,' he remarked.

'Durrand?'

'Yes.'

He laid down the hoe, put on his jacket and took me into the cottage. Soon the whisky bottle was out; and the glasses were on the table.

He guessed what I was thinking.

'Drinking myself into my grave, eh? That's what Owen Stryker told me.'

'Stryker was here last night, wasn't he?'

Lionel frowned. 'Yes, very kind of him, but I'd rather be left alone.'

He fell silent.

'I believe you wanted me to meet someone?' I prompted.

'She's away having tea,' he replied, as he handed me my drink. 'She'll be back presently. It's a girl called Murray. You phoned her mother a while back.'

'Oh! the camper?'

'Yes.'

'What does she want?'

But Lionel told me to wait till I saw her. He was morose and taciturn; conversing with him was hard going.

'Do you mean to stay on here?' I asked.

'For a bit. Until I know who framed me for Geoffrey's murder.'

'I thought you'd fixed on Julia?'

'I'm not so sure now. Caswell was here yesterday morning. He doesn't think it's Julia.'

Conversation died again. Lionel sat staring into his glass. I was wishing Miss Murray would come soon.

Then, in a burst of confidence, Lionel said: 'I asked you down to meet this girl because I need a second opinion. Unless I'm going mad, what she saw that night must mean—'

The door bell rang and Lionel broke off to answer it. He beckoned to me to come out and briefly introduced me to Vera Murray on the doorstep.

She was a tall, rangy girl, brown-eyed and auburn-haired, with a snub nose and lips that looked as if they smiled a lot. She wore slacks and a long, thick woollen sweater and she had a camera slung over her shoulder.

'I'll leave you to get on with it,' said Lionel. 'You'll want to show him what you showed me.'

The girl looked a little perplexed.

'Well, thanks,' she said, 'but before you go, is it all

right if I take a snap of the cottage from the garden? You can't get a proper view from outside.'

Lionel shrugged his consent. He went inside and shut the door.

I followed the girl up the garden to what had been a stretch of lawn; the grass was now eighteen inches high.

'What's the picture for?' I asked, as she removed her camera from its case. It was an expensive model, with all the gadgets.

As I thought it would be, her smile was attractive. 'A souvenir, you might say. I've never been within hailing distance of a murder before. Bridget and I went through half a dozen spools on our trip but we never took the cottage.'

'And is that what you came for today?'

She was busy focusing.

'Not entirely,' she said, after she pressed the button.

She put the camera back in its case. As we walked to the gate, she remarked:

'That's Lionel Wallis, isn't it, that old man?'

'Yes.'

'He looks so ill . . .' She opened the gate and we went out.

In the lane outside a car was parked, an open MG in bright red. In the driving seat sat a youth with the colour section of the *Sunday Times* open on his knee. He vaulted out and came over to us.

Vera introduced him. 'My brother Charles. He drove me down from Reading on condition I paid for his petrol and his meals.'

Charles might have been a twin, the likeness was so marked, but was probably a year or two younger. He also was an undergraduate, though at Reading, he told me.

'Vera's the clever one,' he remarked. 'They wouldn't take me at Oxford. Still, brains aren't everything. Do you think she did it, Dr Slater?'

'It's certainly suspicious, coming back to the scene of the crime like this.'

'Yeah, they all do, don't they?'

'Shut up,' said Vera, laughing. 'Dr Slater, where was Geoffrey Wallis's car parked that night?'

'Don't answer that question,' her brother interjected. 'It's a trap.'

This time there was an edge to Vera's voice: 'Get back to your pretty pictures, Charles. You're just the chauffeur today.'

He grinned, and obediently climbed back into the car and picked up his paper.

Vera repeated the question.

'It was parked there,' I said, 'just where yours is. There was rain later on that night and the car left its tyre-marks when it drove away. I saw them myself. They began just below the cottage gate. So that's where it must have been parked.'

'That's what the detective chap said, the one I saw in Paris, Superintendent Castle—'

'Caswell.'

'All right, Caswell. He said Mr Wallis's car was parked six feet beyond the gate as you come down.'

'That's right.'

'But, you see, that doesn't— Look, come over here.' She set off purposefully down the lane, past her brother's car, and turned into the field through the gap in the hedge lower down. I followed her. She stopped at the spot where her tent had been.

'We'd been sunbathing that afternoon,' she said, when I joined her. 'It was stinking hot, you remember. At six o'clock we boiled a kettle and opened some tins. We had our meal inside the tent, because even Bridget was paralysed by the heat. About twenty past I went out to bury the tins. Bridget was so *fussy* about that.'

The tartness of the remark suggested that the

American girl hadn't proved the ideal companion.

'Well, I just happened to hear this car coming down the lane and stopping. I didn't pay much attention. I'd cut my finger on one of these damned tins and I went down to the stream to bathe it. I was away maybe ten minutes altogether and when I got back to the tent the car was still there. I could see it.'

She paused.

I saw what she was getting at. The hawthorn hedge that bordered the field was patchy, varying in height and in density, and with some clear gaps. Below the cottage, for about ten yards, it was very thick, and Charles's car was totally obscured.

'You're suggesting,' I said, 'that Geoffrey Wallis's car was parked further up the lane at the time you saw it and that it must have been moved down later in the evening?'

'No. I don't believe the car I saw was Mr Wallis's at all.'

I was sceptical. 'You mean there were *two* black Daimlers parked there that night?'

'This one wasn't black and I don't think it was a Daimler.'

'But Superintendent Caswell said—' I began.

'I know. He asked me if I'd seen a car arrive about 6.15 that night and I said yes, and he asked me if it was a black Daimler and I couldn't remember. But he was expecting it to be a black Daimler and I thought and thought about it and eventually I could *see* a black Daimler. Auto-suggestion, I suppose.' She giggled. 'That's worthy of Charles, that pun. However, after the superintendent went away, I began to have my doubts and I've worried ever since. I simply had to come back and have another look. And as soon as I stood here again, the picture of the Daimler faded and I remembered what it was really like. It was green, or pale blue perhaps, certainly not black.'

'What make?' I asked.

'I've no idea. I only saw bits of it through the gap in the

hedge. All I know is it wasn't black and it was parked above the gate, not below it.

'The time was wrong, too,' she added. 'The superintendent persuaded me it was 6.15 when I heard the car arrive. But it wasn't. It was twenty past six, or even a minute or two later.'

'Did you hear the shots? You must have, surely, when you were as close as this to the cottage.'

Vera sighed. 'It's all very well saying "you must have" — the superintendent kept saying it too. But, you see, there was a chap used to go out with a rifle in the woods across there' — she pointed over the river — 'I suppose he was after rabbits. The occasional crack from that rifle became so much a part of the ordinary background of the place that we didn't really notice it, if you see what I mean. I *seem* to remember that, while I was bathing my finger in the stream that night, there were three or four bangs, one right after the other.' She stopped to think about it. 'No, it was bang, pause, bang-bang-bang — like that.'

'Four shots?'

She grinned. 'That's the number the policeman told me I should have heard, so maybe that's why I remember four: I'm a very suggestible girl. But, honestly, I really do believe I heard them. I can remember thinking the poacher or whoever he was must be closer than usual because the reports sounded louder.'

'And that would be about twenty five past six?'

'About then, I should think. A few minutes after the green car arrived.'

We started to walk back across the field towards the lane.

'Did you tell all this to Lionel?' I asked.

She nodded. 'He was in the garden. He heard me talking to Charles, and he came out. He never actually said who he was, though I guessed. He seemed so interested that I told him what was bothering me — about the cars, I mean. I didn't mention the shots. He insisted on phoning for you and when you weren't there he made me promise to come back to meet you.'

'You'll have to tell your story to the police, of course,' I said, as we rejoined her brother at the car.

'I was afraid of that. I was such a dope when I saw the superintendent in Paris. If I phone him tomorrow, will that do.'

'I'd rather you tried to get him tonight. He told me he was to be at the Yard all day. He might still be there.'

But Charles wouldn't hear of phoning. Delighted to have an excuse to visit Scotland Yard, he offered to drive his sister there at once.

'If they let us out,' he said, 'we can still get home before dawn. Jump in, Sis. And remember, that adds three gallons to the bill. Not to speak of supper. You'll have to buy a meal now.'

'All right,' said Vera sweetly, 'you shall have your supper.'

Charles started the engine and, with a final wave of the hand, roared up towards the main road. At once Lionel came over to the gate. He must have been waiting for them to go.

'Well?' he said. 'You know all the answers now, don't you?'

'No,' I replied, avoiding his eye.

'But didn't she tell you about the car?' Surely that can only mean — '

I looked up then. 'I'd rather not talk about it, Lionel,' I said.

I turned away and walked slowly up the lane. At the bend where the road cut round the hill I looked back. Lionel was still at the gate, gazing after me.

At the road junction I turned left into the village. It was nearly seven o'clock. The last rays of the sun lay on the church tower; everything else was in shadow. The chill of an autumn night was moving in.

I turned into the cricket ground, now bleak and deserted, and sat down on a bench. I wondered why I had lied to Lionel. I *did* know the answers now, the essential one anyway. But I didn't want to discuss it until I'd worked out all the ramifications for myself, until the last shadow of doubt was removed.

Curiously, it wasn't the girl Murray's story that had put me on to it. The idea had already been planted by a remark of Jane's at the hospital. At the time I had barely been conscious that something off-beat had been said; but under the surface my brain must have worked on it, for while Vera Murray was talking to me, suddenly I had recognized the discrepancy and at the same moment seen the explanation of it.

One explanation of it, I told myself now. But try as I might, I could think of no other. And presently other facts came to mind that corroborated it. And others. The jigsaw was solved: all the pieces fitted.

I shivered. It was almost dark and it had turned cold. I walked back to Garston.

Stryker's car was still there, I noticed, as I went in the front door. And Durrand must have arrived too. His bicycle was propped against the wall.

I shut the door quietly behind me and tiptoed to the telephone on the hall table. There was a murmur of voices from the living-room, but no one came out.

I dialled Scotland Yard. Caswell was still there.

'Superintendent,' I began, 'I know who murdered Geoffrey Wallis. I've got proof. It's—'

'Dr Slater,' he interrupted, 'I warned you before to be careful on the telephone. Don't say any more, but come straight up here and see me.'

There was a click and I thought he had rung off. But he spoke again: 'Have you got your car?'

'I can borrow one.' Julia's ignition key was on the table

by the phone, where she had left it when she came in.
    'All right, but hurry. And don't say a word to anyone.'
This time he had put down the receiver.

CHAPTER 8

Julia's Morris was still at the front door. I started the
engine, switched on the headlights and, as quietly as I
could, turned the car in a semicircle and set off. Before
the drive plunged down into the avenue of shrubs I glanced
back: there was a reddish glow from the big living-room
window and, higher up, a smaller, brighter square of
light—a bedroom perhaps. All else was black.

    But in the brief second before I turned my eyes back to
the road a narrow pencil of light appeared as someone
opened the front door.

    I concentrated on the mechanics of driving, familiariz-
ing myself with the gear lever, with the feel of the clutch
and the steering.

    It was a moonless night. I had the road to myself as far
as Gleeve, and even beyond it I met only the isolated car.

    In the wide sweep round to Minford a car, travelling at
speed, began to catch up and the white glare of its
headlamps grew larger in my mirror. Presently it was
right on my tail, seemingly impatient to overtake. But
when the bus that had been lumbering towards us had
passed, my follower remained behind me, almost bumper
to bumper.

    I slowed down and waved him on; no result. I acceler-
ated; so did he. And all the time this dazzling, blinding
light in the mirror.

    At Minford cross I turned off towards the council hous-
ing estate. When the car behind swung round after me
my growing suspicion hardened. And moments later all

doubt vanished. The headlights behind me were switched off and when I stole a glance round, a street lamp showed up the car's pale bonnet and the tense face at the wheel.

A shiver of mingled fear and excitement ran down my arms. My phone call to Caswell must have been overheard; the click I had heard was someone replacing the extension in the study.

I twisted about the narrow, featureless streets while I frantically considered what to do. My instinct was to make for Minford Police Station. No one in his senses would attack me in a busy main street.

But I was dealing with someone who wasn't sane, someone desperate and almost certainly armed. To stop the car and get out was the one thing I must not do.

Gradually I edged back towards the main road. My chance came when a local bus, dawdling along ahead, moved across the narrow street to pass a parked car. I put my foot hard down, swung the wheel sharply round and zoomed through the ever-narrowing gap outside the bus. By mounting the pavement and almost scraping the wall I got through. I heard the squeal of brakes as I passed and I had a glimpse of the angry, frightened face of the bus driver. It had worked, though. The road behind me was temporarily blocked and the other car hadn't got through.

I gave the engine everything it had and roared to the intersection, turning left through the red light. I was through the town and out on the London road before I realized I should have used the respite to get to the police station.

Too late now. I had to press on. With the needle hovering on 80, the car was shuddering in anguished protest. As I took one bend too fast and half mounted the bank, I cursed my unfamiliarity with both the car and the road.

Five miles beyond Minford the headlights appeared in the mirror again. We were in a long straight stretch and the gap narrowed fast. Within seconds the car was on my tail and at once the lights moved out to overtake.

As the other car drew level I ducked and simultaneously slammed down on brake and clutch, waiting for the shot and the shattering of glass. Nothing happened. I looked up in time to right the Morris as it headed for the off-side ditch. Ahead of me the rear end of a big black Jaguar disappeared into the night.

I laughed aloud from sheer relief. Eight miles now beyond Minford, fifteen altogether from Garston. Nearly halfway. Perhaps I had got clear.

It crept up on me insidiously, driving on my lights. One moment the road behind me was empty, the next these powerful lights were blazing through my rear window. This time there was no doubt. The car hung there on my tail, waiting . . .

Although it had the edge on me for speed, it made no move to overtake. That was the worst part, not knowing what to expect or when. To every car that passed I made a violent signal with lights and horn: an empty gesture, because anything they might do would be too late.

We were climbing now, quite steeply, and the needle dropped to 60, 50, 45. And now at last the car behind me pulled out.

I knew where we were and what was going to happen. We were approaching Gideon's Crest, and the plan was to edge me over the cliff.

As we levelled out on the shoulder of the hill it had drawn alongside and was pressing me in relentlessly. When I held my ground, the two wings touched and the Morris, the lighter car, spun sharply on to the grass verge. I had a fleeting glimpse of the chasm beneath me before I wrenched the wheel round and skidded back on to the road.

At once the other car closed in again. I tried sudden braking and acceleration but it matched speed for speed. Inch by inch I was forced in, till my nearside wheels were on the grass and less than a foot from the edge. There was no sound but the tormented screaming of the engine, driven to its limit and beyond.

Three hundred yards ahead a wavering band of light lay across the road. Even at that moment, poised on the threshold of eternity, I saw it and wondered about it. The band swung round until it shone up the road towards us; twin bands, really—the lights of a car that had turned in from a junction on the right.

There was room for three cars to pass abreast, especially as one of them—mine—was only half on the road. But the terrifying spectacle of two sets of headlights bearing down on him side by side at speed unnerved or blinded the driver and he veered into the middle of the road.

My pursuer made one last attempt to force me over. Resisting the instinct to brake, I slammed still harder on the accelerator, the wheels teetering now on the very brink.

Then, suddenly, the car at my side was dropping back as the driver, seeing the danger, tried to pull in behind me. Too late. Fractionally after I had swept past the oncoming car there was the sound of an impact, then weird patterns of flashing lights, followed, seconds later, by a tremendous crash. Then silence and darkness.

I pulled up half a mile further on. My hands were shaking and I had to force myself to turn the car and return to the scene. Two men and a woman were standing by a car which lay on its side across the road—an ambulance, as I saw when I got closer. There was no sign of the other car.

The ambulance driver was giving expression to his relief in a stream of profanity, which became more lurid when he learned I was driving the car that had shot past first.

'Shut up,' I said harshly. 'Are any of you hurt?'

One of the men had a superficial cut on his face and the girl—a nurse—had bruised her knee and torn a stocking. Otherwise they were all right.

'And the other car?' I asked, knowing the answer.

It was over the cliff. It had struck the ambulance a glancing blow on the offside wing and had rebounded, out of control, and skidded over the edge.

'He must have been mad,' said the driver, his voice still shaky. 'Or drunk. The pair of you must have been drunk.'

'No, not drunk,' I said.

We walked to the edge and looked down. But all was black.

'Hey, Bill,' the driver called, 'get the torch.'

But it was the girl who brought it. She had recovered more quickly than the two men.

At this point the slope was steep but not sheer. The pale beam of the torch showed the marks where the car had gone over, a gash in the turf at the edge and a bush uprooted a little way down.

'It's a drop of 250 feet,' said the driver. 'Nobody could survive that.' I hoped he was right.

'We'll need to go down and see,' said the nurse.

'It seems a pity to risk our necks for a corpse.' Then accepting the inevitable, he called: 'Bill, get the stretcher out, we're going rock-climbing.'

'Do you want me—' the girl began.

'No, you stay here. Stop the first car that comes along and organize a rescue party. Sherpa Tensing, if you can get him, and ropes.'

'What about this racing driver here?' said Bill, indicating me. 'He could drive to the hospital for help, L-plates and all.'

But they needed my car for its lights. The ambulance, its lights shattered, was a menace to traffic.

'In any case,' I said, 'I'm going down with you.'

The driver's feelings towards me hadn't mellowed.

'Not bloody likely, you're not,' he began. 'We're not—'

'Let him go, George,' said the girl sharply. 'He can

hold the torch for you.' She was very understanding, that nurse.

The descent was uncomfortable rather than dangerous. We scrambled and slithered down, grasping the passing vegetation with our hands as a brake. The stretcher was a problem, but at the steeper bits we simply let it slide ahead of us.

We were down in five minutes, undamaged but for scratched hands. At first we couldn't find the car. We hadn't allowed for its momentum at the impact, which had carried it far forward as it hurtled down.

George had taken the torch now, while Bill and I carried the stretcher. We had walked about a hundred yards along a dried-up river bed, when we saw the green car, upside down, half supported by a stunted tree. The two ambulance men went over to examine it.

'God,' said Bill, 'he must be pinned underneath.'

George bent down and peered. 'I don't think so,' he said. 'He's been thrown clear.'

The torch swivelled in a widening arc round the car. A further exclamation: 'There he is!' A moment's silence, as the torch steadied, then: 'God, it's a woman!'

'Yes,' I muttered to myself, 'it's a woman.'

'She's alive,' added Bill. My heart sank.

I walked over then. She was lying on her back, her face dead white, but unmarked. A trickle of blood was oozing from her mouth.

As I stood there, she opened her eyes. She didn't recognize me, but she was trying to speak. I bent forward.

I caught one word only: 'Chris.'

Anne died half an hour later.

CHAPTER 9

'You'd think there would be an ashtray,' said Caswell.

He had lit his pipe and was irritably waving the blackened match. We were in the matron's office.

Caswell dropped the match on the floor and kicked it under the desk. 'They're taking a hell of a time,' he said.

We were waiting for Julia. When they broke the news to her on the phone, she had insisted on coming to the hospital. Stryker was going to drive her.

Caswell was restless. He had taken a full statement from me, but still he lingered. I could sense the frustration and dissatisfaction that tempered his relief that the case was over.

'Of course,' he said, 'we knew it was her. We just hadn't enough evidence.'

But I didn't want to talk about it.

'How did you get here so quickly?' I asked, heading him off.

'I got a message from Garston. You weren't the only one to suspect her . . . We were on our way to intercept you when that nurse stopped us.'

'Does Jane know?'

He looked guilty. 'No, I'm leaving that to her mother.'

'Where have you taken —?'

'It's in the mortuary here. We'll move it later on, after Mrs Wallis — God, I'm sorry for that woman.'

But I was more concerned about Chris.

There was a knock on the door. Caswell opened it and had a murmured conversation with someone outside. Then with a word of apology he went out.

Now that I was alone the reaction set in. In two minutes I was asleep.

It was Stryker's voice that wakened me. 'So this is where you've been hiding, Professor?'

He came in and sat down, yawning.

'Where's Julia?' I asked him.

'She's with Jane. Chris is there too.'

'I think I'll go and—' I began.

Stryker gazed levelly at me. 'Not yet. Wait till he's quietened Jane. She was hysterical.'

He lit a cigarette. 'You knew it was Anne?' he said.

'Latterly, yes.'

'I should have guessed too. Especially after reading her novel. It's almost a self-portrait. Very revealing—like her father's diary. The same compulsion, I expect.'

'Are you going to publish it?'

He looked at me in surprise. 'Of course! We'd accepted it anyway. It's not impossibly bad—her father's name would have carried it through. Now her own will give it a boost.'

Stryker flicked his ash on the floor.

'Yes, I ought to have guessed,' he went on. 'She was hard as nails and ambitious as hell. But I always was a sucker for a pretty face. I couldn't see behind that. Do you know, I even asked her to marry me once? She might have been tempted, too, but she'd already met Chris. I believe she was really in love with him.'

'Yes,' I said. I wished he would stop.

'But she had to have him on her own terms. She wasn't going to live in poverty. Her father misjudged her when he imagined she'd be content to let Philip Brent disinherit her. They've found Philip, by the way, did you know that?'

'No.'

'Wandering about London making up his mind to tell the world who he really is. My guess is he'll keep it quiet now.'

He opened the window and flicked out the end of his cigarette.

'You knew she'd been in a mental hospital?' he said.

'Who, Anne?'

'Yes. Julia told me going down in the car tonight. She had some sort of breakdown a few years ago and she was away for nearly a year. They kept very quiet about it — gave out she was at a finishing school abroad. Hardly anybody knew the truth.'

Helen had known though. She had got the story wrong at first, when she told me it was Jane who had been ill. Later she had sent me that cryptic message that it was 'the wrong one'.

'I wonder if the police knew,' I mused.

'Oh! yes. Caswell told me tonight they'd known from the beginning. That's why they suspected her. That and the motive. But her alibi stumped them. It was you that gave her it, wasn't it?'

Stryker had got me interested in spite of myself.

'Yes,' I said, 'and I didn't see the flaw till today.'

The mention of cricket during my visit to Jane in hospital had reminded me of my conversation with her on the lawn at Garston on the day of her father's death. She'd had her radio on, and when I was leaving her, the commentator said they were going to start the last over of the day. That meant it still wasn't quite 6.30. Yet when I had wakened, at least a quarter of an hour before, the library clock had been at 6.25. It must have been fifteen minutes fast.

'You mean,' said Stryker, 'that Anne had put it forward to give herself an alibi?'

'I don't think so. She probably felt her plan to incriminate Lionel was so foolproof she didn't need an alibi. All the same she was quick-witted enough to take advantage of one when it was offered. When I told the police Anne had left Garson after 6.25, she confirmed it, though she must have known it wasn't true.'

'Why "must"? She might have been genuinely mistaken too.'

'She met Chris's train at Minford at 6.42. She'd have been bound to realize her mistake if she'd had to cool her heels at the station for a quarter of an hour. Besides, she said she arrived just as the train was getting in. And another thing: Philip Brent said he heard Geoffrey's car go down the drive soon after six, followed, *a minute or two later*, by another, which could only have been Anne's. We know her father left at ten past six. "A minute or two" surely didn't mean twenty minutes.'

'What puzzles me,' said Stryker, 'is why she tried to kill her sister.'

'The diary—'

'Yes, I dare say the missing pages told who Philip was. I can understand why Anne removed them in the first place. But that story was coming into the open anyway. Julia knew it already, so did Durrand. You were just about to dig it up. Why should Anne be so alarmed that Jane had read about it? Julia told me tonight she'd read the diary and there was nothing in it that pointed to Anne in particular.'

'Julia told me that too. But she also said she hadn't seen the last week of the diary. What do you think Geoffrey would be writing about then?'

Stryker took the point. 'Of course! About the plot to drug Lionel and get the confession back from him.'

'Yes. And since Geoffrey was nothing if not frank in his diary, he'd mention who his collaborator was, which was something Anne would have to suppress at all costs. Incidentally, you were there when Jane announced she'd read the missing pages. Supposing you'd been the murderer, how would you have reacted?'

'Well, she was pretty vague, wasn't she? I'd have wanted to be absolutely certain she really had read the bit about me before I chanced a second murder.'

'Quite. Well, when Jane was talking to me about it today, she said that, to make the pretence of having read the diary more convincing, she'd added the other bits "about Uncle Lionel and all that". Did you hear her mention Lionel that night?'

'I'm sure she didn't.'

'No. Yet you remember she went straight upstairs to her room and nobody saw her again till she left for her party. Except Anne. She went upstairs with her. That's when Jane must have made up the bit about Lionel. No doubt Anne pressed her to say what she'd read in the diary. And her imagination must have gone too near the truth for her sister's peace of mind . . .'

I was wound up now. I went on to tell him about the green car that had been seen arriving at Lionel's cottage at 6.20 on the night of the murder.

'Anne had a green Consul,' I pointed out, 'and the time fitted, now that I knew she'd left Garston about 6.15 and not 6.30.'

Stryker nodded. 'But, you know,' he said, 'the most glaring pointer of all was the fact that Geoffrey had confided in someone about the plot to deal with Lionel. Anne was the only one he trusted. We ought to have seen that. It had to be Anne.'

I remembered the inscription Geoffrey had written in the book I had seen in Anne's flat.

'Yes,' I said sadly, 'it had to be Anne.'

There was a long silence. When Stryker spoke again, his tone was brisker.

'Well,' he said, 'you've got the ending for your book now, Professor. and you couldn't ask for a more dramatic one.'

His words jarred on me. Even tonight his business instinct was at work.

Before I could answer, the door opened and Chris came in.

'Well,' said Stryker, 'I expect you two will want to talk.'
It was a question rather than a statement. When neither
of us answered, he stumped out.

Chris came over and sat down.

'I'm glad you're all right, Dad,' he said.

'How's Julia?' I asked.

'Bearing up. It's Jane that's the problem.'

He spoke as if Jane were *his* problem. And when I looked
at him, I wondered whether that might not be what he
meant.

'Chris,' I began, trying to find the right words, 'Anne
wasn't—'

'Don't sympathize, Dad. I don't need sympathy.'

His voice was harsh.

Then he said, more quietly: 'I knew about Anne. Oh! I
don't mean I knew she'd murdered her father. At least,
not till tonight, when she went dashing off after you . . .'

So it was Chris who had phoned Caswell from Garston.

'. . . but I knew quite early on that she was no good.
She was completely wrapped up in herself. I didn't love
her. The only thing was, she needed me and—well, I'd
seen for myself what can happen to someone like that. I
couldn't leave her.'

He was referring to Helen. He was condemning me for
deserting her. I wished he didn't have such a sense of personal responsibility and involvement. Now it would be
Jane, no doubt; he'd feel he was the only one who could
help her.

But he was continuing, his voice still hard and un-
friendly: 'Never mind, Dad, your name's made now.
With a climax like that, the book ought to hit the
jackpot.'

'I'm not writing it, Chris,' I said quietly. 'I couldn't
write it now. You came in just as I was about to tell
Stryker.'

The tautness in his face relaxed.

After a while he said: 'I'm going to see Mother tomorrow. Would you like to come?' His off-hand tone didn't deceive me.

Chris was coming back to me, but at a price. I decided I would pay the price.

'Yes,' I said. 'I'll come.'

The number of books that may be
drawn at one time by the card holder
is governed by the reasonable needs of
the reader and the material on hand.

Books for junior readers are subject
to special rules.